Natasha found herself facing Mario.

"You've danced with everyone else," he observed. "Will it ever be my turn?"

"Not until you ask me."

"No," he said. "I'm not going to ask you."

But as he spoke, his arm went around her waist in a grip too firm for her to resist, even if she had wanted to.

Once before they had danced together. One night in Venice, when they had been having supper at an outdoor café in St. Mark's Square, a band had started to play, and before she'd known it she'd been waltzing in his arms.

"Is this all right?" he'd whispered.

"I'll let you know later," she had teased.

It had lasted only a few minutes, and she had promised herself that one day she would dance with him again. But the next day they had broken up, and it had never happened again. Until now.

It was unnerving to feel his arms about her, his hand on her waist, holding her close. Her heart was beating softly but fervently. She glanced at him, trying to know if he felt the same. Would he invite her to dance with him again?

Dear Reader,

Verona has always been one of my favorite Italian cities. Being Italian by marriage, I've visited many places in that lovely country: Venice, Rome, Florence. They are all beautiful, but Verona has something else: the lingering attraction of the world's best known and most heartbreaking love affair—*Romeo and Juliet*.

Some of the story is legend, but long ago there really were two young people who sacrificed their lives for their love, and their tragic story moves people to this day. Their story stayed with me when I went to Verona, walking the picturesque streets and going to see Juliet's house. There her statue stands, gazing at the visitors who seek to share her secrets.

Natasha, my heroine, originally goes to Verona to work, but before long she is enfolded in the magic of the legend. At times her own love seems equally fated to end sadly, but she has the courage to cling on and help her lover achieve the happiness that was always meant to be.

Juliet would have been proud of her.

Lucy Gordon

Reunited with Her Italian Ex

Lucy Gordon

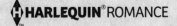

Recycling programs
for this product may
not exist in your area.

ISBN-13: 978-0-373-74330-8

Reunited with Her Italian Ex

First North American Publication 2015

Copyright © 2015 by Lucy Gordon

Printed in U.S.A.

www.Harlequin.com

Lucy Gordon cut her writing teeth on magazine journalism, interviewing many of the world's most interesting men. She's had many unusual experiences, which have often provided the background for her books. Once, while staying in Venice, she met a Venetian who proposed in two days, and they've been married ever since. Naturally this has affected her writing, in which romantic Italian men tend to feature strongly. Two of her books have won a Romance Writers of America RITA® Award. You can visit her website at lucy-gordon.com.

Books by Lucy Gordon

HARLEQUIN ROMANCE

Not Just a Convenient Marriage

The Falcon Dynasty

Rescued by the Brooding Tycoon
Miss Prim and the Billionaire
Plain Jane in the Spotlight
Falling for the Rebel Falcon
The Final Falcon Says I Do

The Larkville Legacy

The Secret That Changed Everything

Visit the Author Profile page
at Harlequin.com for more titles

PROLOGUE

VENICE, THE MOST romantic city in the world.
That was what people said, and Natasha
was becoming convinced that it was true.
Where else could she have met the man of her
dreams within hours of arriving, and known
so soon that she was his and he simply must
become hers?

Sitting in a café by a small canal, she
looked out at the sun glittering on the water.
Nearby she could see a gondola containing
a young man and woman, wrapped in each
other's arms.

Just like us, she thought, recalling her first
gondola ride in the arms of the man who had
changed the world in moments.

Mario Ferrone, young, handsome, with
dancing eyes and a rich chuckle that seemed
to encompass the world. She'd met Mario
just after she'd arrived in Venice on a well-
earned holiday. He'd insisted on showing

her the city. As his brother owned the hotel where she was staying, she'd briefly thought this a professional service, but that idea soon changed. There was an instant attraction between them, and nothing had ever seemed more wonderful than the time they spent together.

Until then, there had been little in her life that could be called romance. She was slim, pretty, humorous, with no difficulty attracting admirers. But where men were concerned she had an instinctive defensiveness.

It went back to her childhood, when her father had abandoned his wife and ten-year-old daughter for another woman. Until that moment Natasha's life had been happy. Her father had seemed to adore her as she adored him. But suddenly he was gone, never to get in touch again.

Never trust a man, her mother had told her. *They'll always let you down.*

She'd been content to heed the warning until Mario came into her life and everything turned upside down.

Her own reactions confused her. Her heart was drawn to Mario as never before to any other man. Sometimes her mother's voice echoed in her mind.

No man can be trusted, Natasha. Remember that.

But Natasha felt certain that Mario was different to all other men—more honest, more trustworthy, more faithfully loving.

Last night he'd kissed her with even greater fervour than before, murmuring, 'Tomorrow I want to…' Then he'd stopped, seeming confused.

'Yes?' she'd whispered. 'What do you want?'

'I can't tell you now…but tomorrow everything will be different. Goodnight, *mi amore.*'

Now here she was in the café where they often met, waiting for him to appear and transform her world yet again.

She almost ached with the yearning to know what he'd meant by 'everything will be different'. Was he going to propose marriage? Surely he must.

Oh, please hurry, she thought. How could Mario keep her on tenterhooks when it mattered so much?

Suddenly, she heard his voice call, 'Natasha!' Looking up, she saw him walking by the canal, waving to her from a distance.

'Sorry I'm late,' he said, joining her at the table. 'I got held up.'

She had a strange feeling that he was on edge.

'Is everything all right?' she asked.

'It will be, very soon,' he said.

His eyes never left her and every moment her conviction grew that tonight they were going to take the next step—whatever it might be.

He took her hand. 'There's something I've been trying to tell you for days but—'

'Trying? Is it so hard to tell me?'

'It could be.' His eyes met hers. 'Some things just aren't easy to say.'

Her heart was beating with anticipation and excitement. She knew what he was going to say, and she longed to hear it.

'That depends how much you want to say them,' she whispered, leaning close so that her breath brushed his face. 'Perhaps you don't really want to say this.'

'Oh, yes, you don't know how much it matters.'

But I do know, she thought happily. He was going to tell her how much she meant to him. In a moment her life would be transformed.

She took his hand in hers, sending him a silent message about her willingness to draw closer to him.

'Go on,' she whispered.

He hesitated and she regarded him, puzzled. Was it really so hard for him to reach out to her?

'Natasha—I want to tell you—'

'Yes—yes—tell me.'

'I'm not good at this—'

'You don't need to be good at it,' she urged, tightening her clasp on his hand. 'Just say it—'

'Well—'

'Traitor!'

The screamed word stunned them both. Natasha looked up to see a woman standing by the table, glaring at them. She was in her thirties, voluptuous, and would have been beautiful but for the look of livid hatred she cast on Mario.

'Traitor!' she screamed. *'Liar! Deceiver!'*

Mario's face was tense and pale as Natasha had never seen it before. He rose and confronted the woman, speaking angrily in Italian and pointing for her to leave. She screamed back at him in English. Then turned to Natasha.

'It's about time you knew what he is really like. One woman isn't enough for him.'

She raved on until Mario drew her into a corner, arguing with her vigorously. Natasha could no longer hear the words but there was no mistaking the intensity between them. The dark-haired woman's rage grew with every moment.

'He's a liar and a cheat,' she screamed in perfect English.

'Mario,' Natasha said, 'who is this woman? Do you really know her?'

'Oh, yes, he knows me,' the woman spat. 'You wouldn't believe how well he knows me.'

'Tania, that's enough,' Mario said, white-faced. 'I told you—'

'Oh, yes, you told me. Traitor! Traitor! *Traditore!*'

For a moment Natasha was tempted to thrust herself between them and tell Mario what she thought of him in no uncertain terms. But then her impetuous temper flared even higher, driving her to a course of action even more fierce and desperate. While they were still absorbed in their furious encounter, she fled.

She ran every step of the way to the hotel, then up to her room, pausing at the desk to demand her bill. Nothing mattered but to get away from here before Mario returned. It had all been a deception. She'd believed in him because she'd wanted to believe, and she should have known better. Now she was paying the price.

'You were right,' she muttered to her mother's ghost. 'They're all the same.'

The ghost was too tactful to say *I told you so*, but she was there in Natasha's consciousness as she finished packing, paid her bill and fled.

She took a boat taxi across the water to the mainland, and from there she switched to a motor taxi.

'Airport,' she told the driver tensely.

Oh, Mario, she thought as the car roared away. *Traitor.*

Traditore.

CHAPTER ONE

Two years later...

'I'M SORRY, NATASHA, but the answer's no, and that's final. You just have to accept it.'

Natasha's face was distorted by anger as she clutched the phone.

'Don't tell me what I have to do,' she snapped into the receiver. 'You said you were eager for anything I wrote—'

'That was a long time ago. Things have changed. I can't buy any more of your work. Those are my orders.'

Natasha took a shuddering breath as yet another rejection slammed into her.

'But you're the editor,' she protested. 'Surely it's you who gives the orders.'

'The magazine's owner tells us what to do and that's final. You're out. Finished. Goodbye.'

The editor hung up, leaving Natasha staring at the phone in fury and anguish.

'Another one?' asked a female voice behind her. 'That's the sixth editor who's suddenly turned against you after buying your work for ages.'

Natasha turned to her friend Helen, who was also her flatmate.

'I can't believe it,' she groaned. 'It's like there's a spider at the centre of a web controlling them all, telling them to freeze me out.'

'But there is. Surely you know that. The spider's name is Elroy Jenson.'

It's true, Natasha thought reluctantly. Jenson owned a huge media empire that until recently had provided her with a good living. But he'd taken a fancy to her and pursued her relentlessly, ignoring her pleas to be left alone. Finally he'd gone too far, forcing her to slap his face hard enough to make him yell. One of his employees had seen them and spread the story.

'Everyone knows you made him look a fool,' Helen said sympathetically. 'So now he's your enemy. It's a pity about that quick temper of yours, Natasha. You had every right to be angry but…well…'

'But I should have paused before I clobbered him. I should have been calm and controlled and thought about the future. Hah!'

'Yes, I know it sounds ironic, but look at the price you've paid.'

'Yes,' Natasha said with a heavy sigh.

As a freelance journalist her success had been dazzling. Magazines and newspapers clamoured for her sassy, insightful articles.

Until now.

'How can one man have so much power?' she groaned.

'Perhaps you need to go abroad for a while,' Helen suggested. 'Until Jenson forgets all about you.'

'That would be difficult—'

'It needn't be. The agency found me a job in Italy, doing publicity. It would mean going out there for a while. I was about to call them and say they'd have to find someone else, but why don't you go instead?'

'But I can't just… That's a mad idea.'

'Sometimes madness is the best way. It could be just what you need now.'

'But I don't speak Italian.'

'You don't have to. It's an international thing, promoting the city all over the world.'

'It's not Venice, is it?' Natasha asked, suddenly tense.

'No, don't worry. I know you wouldn't want to go to Venice. It's Verona, the city of *Romeo and Juliet*. Some of that story is real, and tourists love to see Juliet's balcony and other places where different scenes are set. So a group of luxury hotel owners have clubbed together to create some publicity for the place. Of course, I know you're not exactly a fan of romance—'

'It doesn't bother me,' Natasha said quickly. 'I'm not going into retreat just because one man— Well, anyway—'

'Fine. So why don't you take this job?'

'But how can I? It's yours.'

'I really wish you would. I accepted it impulsively because I'd had a row with my boyfriend. I thought we were finished, but we've made up and it would really suit me if you went instead of me.'

'But if they're expecting you—'

'I've been dealing with the agency. I'll put you in touch with them and sing your praises. Natasha, you can't let your life be ruled by a man you haven't seen for two years. Especially when he was a cheating rogue. Your words, not mine.'

'Yes,' she murmured. 'I said that. And I meant it.'

'Then go. Put Mario behind you and put Elroy behind you, too. Seize your chance for a fresh start.'

Natasha took a deep breath. 'All right,' she said. 'I'll do it.'

'Fine. Now, let's get started.'

Helen logged on to her computer and contacted the agency. Moments later, Natasha was reading an email, written in efficient English, offering her the assignment and giving her instructions:

You will be dealing with Giorgio Marcelli. The hotel owners employ him to handle publicity. He looks forward to welcoming you to Verona.

'You see, it's a no-brainer,' Helen said. 'I'll leave you to have a think.'

She departed.

Left alone, Natasha stared out of the window, trying to decide what to do. Despite what Helen said, it wasn't easy to make up her mind.

'Not Venice,' she had asserted and Helen had reassured her, because she knew that nothing would persuade Natasha ever to go back to that beautiful romantic city where her heart had been broken.

Natasha thought back to herself as a very young woman, haunted by her mother's warnings never to trust a man. She had pursued a successful career, devoting her time to her writing, avoiding emotional relationships. Of course she could flirt and enjoy male company. But never for very long. Eventually distrust would make her back away from any man who attracted her.

She'd been glad of it, sure that caution would protect her from suffering her mother's fate. On that she had been resolved.

Until she'd met Mario.

He had affected her as no other man ever had. Together they had walked the streets of Venice, drifting by the canals. In one tiny alley he'd drawn her into the shadows for their first kiss. Despite her attempts to obliterate the memory, it still lived in her now.

Her whole body had responded to him, coming alive in ways she had never dreamed of before. She could sense the same in him, although every instinct told her that he was an experienced lover. Wherever they went, women had thrown admiring glances at him and regarded Natasha with envy. She'd guessed they were thinking how lucky she was to be sharing his bed. That day had never come, although several times Natasha had been on the verge of giving in to temptation.

As the day of her departure neared, Mario had begged her to stay with him a little longer. Blissfully happy, she had agreed.

Even now, two years later, remembering that happiness was the most painful thing of all, despite her frantic attempts to banish it from her memory, her heart, her life.

She imagined his face when he'd returned to the table and found her gone.

Vanished into thin air, she thought. *As far as he's concerned I no longer exist, and he no longer exists to me.*

In fact, the man she'd believed him to be had never existed. That was what she had to face.

Bitterly, she replayed the scene. She'd been so sure that he was about to declare his feelings, but when he'd said, 'There's something I've been trying to tell you for days,' he'd actually been planning to dump her.

He'd probably spent the afternoon with Tania, perhaps in her bed.

She thought he was being unfaithful to her with me. In fact he was being unfaithful to both of us. That's the kind of man he is.

After fleeing from Venice, Natasha had done everything she could to disappear for ever, changing her email address and phone number.

But one email from him had just managed to get through before the old address was cut off:

Where did you vanish to? What happened? Are you all right?

Yes, she thought defiantly. *I'm all right. I got rid of the only person who could hurt me. And nobody is ever going to do that to me again.*

She'd never replied to Mario, merely instructing the server to block his emails. Then she'd moved in with Helen. If he came to her old flat he would find the door locked against him as firmly as her heart was locked against him.

At night she would lie awake, dismayed by the violence of her response. He had touched her emotions with an intensity that warned her to escape while there was still time. That way lay the only safety.

Oh, Mario, she thought. *Traitor. Traditore.*

Since then she'd devoted herself to work, making such an impression that she came to the attention of Elroy Jenson. The media magnate had propositioned her, certain that a mere freelance journalist would never refuse him. When she did refuse he couldn't believe it, persisting until she was forced to slap his face and bring her successful career to a sudden end.

After that, her life had been on a downward spiral. Her income had collapsed. Now she could barely afford the small rent she paid on the room she rented from Helen.

The time had come for firm action. And if that meant leaping into the unknown, she would do it. The unknown had its attractions, and suddenly she was ready for anything.

She exchanged brisk emails with Giorgio, the publicity manager. He informed her that she would be staying at the Dimitri Hotel and a driver would meet her at the airport. Two days later she embarked on the journey that might lead to a triumphant new life, or a disaster. Either way, she was venturing into the unknown.

During the flight to Verona she kept her mind firmly concentrated on work. *Romeo and Juliet* was a story that had long touched the world: two young people who fell in love despite the enmity of their families. In the end, they chose to die rather than live without each other.

Legend said that Shakespeare's play was based on real events. The lovers had really lived and died. It would be her job to immerse herself in the story and entice the world to join her.

The driver was at the airport, holding up a placard bearing the words 'Dimitri Hotel'. He greeted her with relief, and ushered her into the car for the three-mile journey to Verona.

'The hotel is in the centre of town,' he said. 'Right next to the river.'

Verona was an ancient, beautiful city. Delighted, she gazed out of the window, enchanted by the hints of another, mysterious age. At last they drew up outside a large elaborate building.

'Here we are. Dimitri Hotel,' the driver said.

As she entered the elegant lobby, a man came forward. He was in his sixties, heavily built, with a plump, smiling face. He greeted her in English.

'The agency told me there had been a change of plan,' he said. 'Apparently the original candidate couldn't make it, but they say you have excellent credentials.'

'Thank you. I'm an experienced journalist. I hope I can live up to your expectations.'

'I'm sure you will. I'm very glad you're here. I promised the President the lady would be here for him tonight and it's never good to disappoint him.'

He gave a comical shudder which made Natasha ask, 'Is he a difficult man? Scary?'

'Sometimes. Mostly he's very determined. People don't cross him if they can help it. He only bought this hotel just under two years ago and set about changing everything practically the first day. There's been a massive redecoration, and the staff has been reorganised to suit him. Everything has to be done his way. Nobody argues.'

'You called him the President.'

'President of the *Comunità*. It was his idea that a group of hotel owners of Verona, the *Comunità*, should all work together. They thought it would be an easy-going organisation but he said it needed leadership. The others just did as he suggested and named him President.

'A while back one of the other owners thought of challenging him for the top job, but he was "persuaded" not to. Nobody knows how, but neither was anyone surprised.

'When he gives his orders we jump to attention, especially me, because he could fire me any time he likes. I'm only telling you so that you'll take care not to offend him.

'We'll dine with him tonight and tomorrow you will meet all the *Comunità* members. They're looking forward to having you spread the word about our lovely city.'

'But isn't the word already out? Surely *Romeo and Juliet* is the most famous love story in the world?'

'True, but we need to make people realise how they can become involved. Now, I'll show you to your room.'

On their way up they passed two men having a noisy argument. One was clearly in command, yelling, *'Capisci? Capisci?'* so fiercely that the other backed off.

'What does that word mean?' Natasha asked curiously. 'It really scared the other guy.'

'It means "Do you understand?"' Giorgio laughed. 'It's really just a way of saying "You'll do as I say. *Get it?*"'

'It sounds useful.'

'It can be, if you're trying to make it clear who's in charge.' He grinned. 'I've had it said to me a few times. Here's your room.'

Like the rest of the place, her room was elegant and luxurious. A huge window looked out over the river, where the sun shone on the water. The atmosphere seemed peaceful and she took a deep contented breath.

When she'd unpacked she took a shower and began work on her appearance. For this meeting she was going to look her best.

She was attractive so not too much effort was required. Her blue eyes were large and expressive. Her blonde hair had just a touch of red that showed in some lights but not in others.

Natasha pinned her hair high on her head, suggesting businesslike severity. Usually, she preferred to let it flow, curved and luscious about her shoulders in a more relaxed way.

But not tonight, she mused, studying herself in the mirror. *Tonight I'm a businesswoman, here to earn a living.*

She fixed her hair firmly away from her face until she felt it conveyed the serious message she intended. Giorgio had warned her that the owner was a man to be reckoned with, but she could deal with that. She'd meet him on his own ground, a woman to be reckoned with.

'I did the right thing in coming here,' she whispered. 'Everything's going to be fine.'

In Venice, a city where most of the roads were water, motor cars could only come as far as Piazzale Roma, the car park on the edge of town. In the glowing heat of a sunny day, Mario Ferrone went to collect his car, accompanied by his brother Damiano.

'It sounds like your hotel is doing really well,' Damiano said. 'You've got a great future ahead of you.'

'I think I just might have,' Mario said, grinning.

'No doubt,' Damiano said cheerfully. 'After all, look who taught you.'

This was a reference to Damiano's successful career as the owner of several hotels. Mario had learned the trade working in many of them and had finally become ambitious for his own establishment.

'That's right, I learned from the best,' Mario said. 'And having a place in Verona is a help. Several of us hoteliers have got together to promote the *Romeo and Juliet* angle.'

'The city of lovers,' Damiano said wryly. 'That should suit you. You'd hardly believe some of the tales I've heard about you.'

'Not recently,' Mario said quickly.

'No, you've settled down these last couple of years, but before that I remember you gave a whole new meaning to the term "bad boy".'

'Most of us do before we find the right woman,' Mario pointed out.

'True. I wasn't a saint before I met Sally. But you haven't met your "Sally", so what made you suddenly become virtuous?'

'Virtuous? Me? No need to insult me.'

Damiano grinned. 'So is it just a smoke-screen?'

'No. I really have changed, not necessarily for the better.'

'Don't say that. You're much improved— quieter, more serious, more grown-up…'

'More suspicious and demanding, nastier sometimes,' Mario said quietly.

'Hey, why do you put yourself down?'

'Perhaps because I know myself better than anyone else does. I'm not the nice guy I used to be—if I ever was.'

'So what made it happen?'

Mario clapped him on the shoulder. 'Don't ask me. It's a long story, and one that—well, that I don't care to think of too often. Let's leave it. I'd better be going. Giorgio has hired a journalist he says will be brilliant at promoting the *Romeo and Juliet* angle. I'm meeting her for dinner when I get back tonight.'

'Best of luck. Goodbye, brother.'

They embraced each other. Damiano stood back, waving as Mario turned out of the car park and across the causeway that led to the mainland.

From Venice to Verona was nearly seventy-five miles. During the journey Mario reflected wryly on his brother's words. Damiano didn't know that one of the turning points in Mario's life had been Damiano's marriage to Sally, four years earlier. Mario had been strongly attracted to Sally, something he'd had to fight. He'd fought it by working in Damiano's hotels in Rome, Florence, Milan, only rarely returning to Venice.

Until then his life had been free and easy. He was young, charming and handsome, with no trouble attracting women. He'd had many girlfriends. Too many, he now realised.

He'd returned to Venice for the birth of his brother's son and found, to his relief, that Sally no longer attracted him, except as a sister. He'd settled into a life of work and pleasure.

Then had come the other great turning point in his life, when he'd met the one woman who could make a difference, drive away the loneliness and give his existence meaning.

Fantasy dictated that she should feel the same and throw herself into his arms. The bitter reality was that she had walked out on him, slamming the door in his face, condemning him to a bleak isolation that was all the worse because he had glimpsed a glorious future, and come so close to embracing it.

Buying the hotel two years ago had been a lucky chance. The owner was eager to sell and accepted a discounted price, and now Mario felt that he was headed for success and independence. If he did nothing else in his life he would triumph in this, he vowed to himself. With that hope to guide him he could banish the pain and bleakness of the last two years.

At last he reached the hotel. Giorgio came to the entrance to greet him.

'It's all set up,' he said.

'Has the lady arrived?'

'Yes, an hour ago. She's not who I was expecting. The agency made a last-minute change, but she seems serious and professional.'

'I can't wait to meet her.' As they walked across the elegant lobby, Mario looked around him at the place he was beginning to regard as his kingdom. 'You know, I have the best possible feeling about this,' he said. 'We're on the right road, and we're going to reach a great destination.'

'One where the money is,' Giorgio supplied with a grin.

'Of course, but that's not the only thing. Somehow, everything is beginning to feel right.'

'That's the spirit. Get settled in and then I'll introduce you to... Mario? Mario, is something wrong?'

But Mario didn't hear him. His attention had been drawn to the great staircase that led to the next floor. He was staring at it like a man stunned. A young woman was walking

down the stairs. She moved slowly, pausing
to look at the paintings on the wall, so that at
first she didn't seem to notice Mario standing
by the bottom step.

When her eyes came to rest on Mario she
stopped suddenly, as if unable to believe her
eyes.

A terrible stillness came over Natasha as she
looked down the staircase, trying to understand what was happening. It was impossible
that Mario should be standing there, staring
up at her with a thunderstruck expression.

Impossible.

And yet it was true. He was there, looking like a man who'd seen a nightmare come
to life.

She tried to move but the stillness enveloped her. Now he was climbing the stairs
slowly, as though unwilling to approach her
too quickly or come too close. When he spoke
it was uneasily.

'I believe…we've met before.'

A dozen answers clamoured in her head,
but at last she heard herself say, 'No, never.'

That took him off-guard, she could see.
While he struggled for a reply, Giorgio's voice
reached them from the bottom of the stairs.

'Aha! I see you two are getting acquainted.'
Waving cheerfully, he climbed up to join them.

'Natasha, let me introduce Mario Ferrone, the owner of the hotel and President of the *Comunità*. Mario, this is Natasha Bates, the lady who's going to tell the world about Verona.'

Mario inclined his head formally. '*Buongiorno, signorina.* It's a pleasure to meet you.'

'How do you do?' she said, nodding towards him.

'Let's go and eat,' Giorgio said, 'and we can have a good talk.'

Downstairs, a table was laid for them in a private room overlooking the river. Giorgio led Natasha to the chair nearest the window and drew it out for her.

A waiter hurried in, eager to serve the hotel's owner. His manner was respectful and she was reminded of Giorgio's words:

'When he gives his orders we all jump to attention…'

She'd known him as a cheeky playboy, always ready to laugh and use his charm. It was hard to see the man he'd been then as the stern authoritarian that Giorgio described now. But his face had changed, growing slightly thinner, firmer, more intense. Even his smile had something reserved about it.

Turning her eyes to him briefly, she caught him glancing at her and realised that he was studying her too. What did he see? Had she also changed, becoming older, sterner, less relaxed? Probably. Perhaps she should be glad, for it would make her stronger. And she was going to need strength now.

Giorgio claimed her attention, filling her wine glass, smiling at her with an air of deferential admiration. He had probably been handsome in his youth, and still had the air of a practised flirt.

'How much were you told about this job?' he asked her.

'Only that some Verona hotel owners had got together to promote the city's connection with *Romeo and Juliet*,' Natasha said.

'That's right. It's already well promoted by the council, which works hard to bring tourists here. But the hotel owners wanted to enjoy a bit more of the spotlight, so they formed the Comunità di Verona Ospitalità so that they could make the most of being in the town that saw the greatest love story in the world.

'Shakespeare didn't invent *Romeo and Juliet*. There really were two families called Montague and Capulet, and they did have children who fell in love, and died. It happened in the early fourteenth century. In the next two hundred years the story was told and retold, until finally Shakespeare based his play on the legend. Tourists come here to see "Juliet's balcony" and imagine the balcony scene happening there.'

'Which it didn't,' Mario observed drily. 'The house belonged to a family called Capello, but the council added the balcony less than a hundred years ago.'

'But if everyone knows that—' Natasha mused.

'They know it but they ignore it,' Giorgio said cheerfully. 'People are often tempted to believe only what they want to.'

'How true,' Natasha murmured. 'That's why we're all so easily taken in.'

She didn't look directly at Mario as she said these words, but she had a sense that he was watching her with an air of tension that matched her own.

'And that's what we can make use of,' Giorgio said. 'Juliet's balcony, Juliet's tomb, where Romeo killed himself because he couldn't bear life without her, and where she killed herself for the same reason. Is it true? It is if we want it to be.'

'Oh, yes,' Natasha mused. 'True if we want

it to be—until one day we have to face the fact that it isn't true, however much we want it.'

'But that's show business,' Giorgio said. 'Creating a fantasy that makes people happy.'

'And what more could we want than that?' Mario asked.

He raised his glass and drank from it, seemingly oblivious to her. But the next moment he said, 'Tell us something about yourself, *signorina*.'

She turned her head, meeting his eyes directly. 'What did you say?'

'I said I'd like to know about you. I'm sure there is much you could tell us. What are your family obligations? Are you free to live in Verona for several weeks, or is there someone at home who will be missing you?'

'I suppose there must be,' Giorgio said. He assumed a chivalrous air. 'This is a lovely lady. She must have crowds of men following her.'

'That doesn't mean that I let them catch up,' Natasha teased.

'Some women are very good at keeping out of sight,' Mario said.

'Of course,' Giorgio agreed. 'That's the secret. Let them chase after you, but don't let any of them get close enough to know what you're thinking and feeling.' He kissed her hand gallantly. '*Signorina*, I can see you're an expert in keeping your admirers wondering.'

'But just what are they wondering?' Mario asked. 'Will any of them arrive here to assert his "rights"?'

'What rights?' Giorgio demanded. 'She's not married.'

'That's irrelevant,' Mario observed. 'You have only to study *Romeo and Juliet* to see that men and women make that decision within a few moments of meeting. And nobody dares get in their way.'

'When people fear betrayal they can get violent,' Giorgio agreed.

Natasha nodded. 'And if they know for sure that they've been betrayed, there's no knowing how far they'll go to make someone sorry,' she mused, letting her glance rest on Mario.

She was glad to see that he understood the silent message. Before her eyes he flinched and averted his gaze. When he spoke again it was in a voice so defiantly businesslike that it told its own story.

'So we can expect a jealous lover to follow you out here?' he said curtly.

She faced him, reading the chilly hostility in his eyes, answering it with her own.

'On the contrary. You can be certain that

nothing will make me leave before my work is finished,' she said calmly. 'Unlike some people, I'm honest about my intentions. I don't make promises and break them.'

'That's not exactly what I asked.'

No, she thought. *You asked whether I'd had the nerve to replace you with another man.*

She gave him her most confident smile, as though his questions merely amused her.

'Let me assure you that I am free,' she said. 'No man tells me what to do, and if anyone tried—' she leaned closer to him '—I would make him regret that he ever knew me.' She added significantly, 'I'm good at that.'

'I believe you,' he said.

Giorgio glanced at them curiously. 'Hey, do you two already know each other?'

'No,' Natasha said quickly, before Mario could speak.

'Really? I feel like I'm watching a fencing match.'

'It's more fun that way,' she said lightly. 'Go on telling me about Verona. Unless, of course, Signor Ferrone has decided he doesn't wish to employ me. In which case I'll just pack up and go. Shall I?'

She made as if to rise but Mario's hand detained her.

'No need for that,' he said harshly. 'Let's get on with the job.'

'Yes, that's the only thing that matters,' she said, falling back into the chair.

For a moment he kept his hand on her arm. 'So we are agreed? You will stay?'

'I will stay.'

CHAPTER TWO

MARIO RELEASED HER. 'As long as we understand each other.'

Natasha drew a tense breath as the bitter irony of those words swept over her. They had never understood each other. Nor could they ever, except on the lines of mutual defensiveness and mistrust.

She turned to Giorgio, assuming her most businesslike tone.

'So it's time I consulted with the Publicity Manager. Tell me, what are my instructions?'

'We must go on a trip around Verona,' he said, 'studying all the significant places. Especially the balcony. These days you can even get married in Juliet's house. And afterwards the bride and groom always come out onto the balcony for the photographs.'

'Useful,' she said, taking out her notebook and beginning to write. 'The balcony scene is the most famous part of the story.'

'Yes, people love to imagine Juliet standing there, yearning for her lover, saying, "Romeo, Romeo, where art thou Romeo?"'

'She doesn't say "where",' Natasha objected. 'She says "Wherefore". It means "Why?" She's saying "Why did you have to be Romeo, a Montague, and my enemy?" In Shakespeare's time, if you wanted to know why someone had behaved in a certain way, you'd say—' she assumed a dramatic attitude '"—Wherefore did thou do this, varlet?"'

'Varlet?' Giorgio queried.

'It means rascal. You'd say it to someone who'd behaved disgustingly.'

Giorgio gave a crack of laughter. 'I must remember that. Rascal—*briccone*.'

'Or *traditore*,' Natasha observed lightly.

'Aha! So you know some Italian words?' Giorgio said eagerly.

'One or two,' she said with a fair assumption of indifference.

'I'd give a lot to know how you learned that particular one,' he said cheekily.

'You'll just have to wonder,' she chuckled.

Mario wasn't looking at her. He seemed completely occupied with his wine.

A man appeared in the doorway, signalling to Giorgio.

'I've got to leave you for a moment,' he

said. 'But I'll be back.' He laid a hand on Natasha's shoulder. 'Don't go away. I have a very good feeling about this.'

'So have I,' she said. 'I'll be right here.'

When Giorgio had gone, Mario refilled her wine glass.

'Be cautious about Giorgio,' he said. 'He turns on the charm as part of his trade.'

'But of course,' she said cheerfully. 'It's a form of show business. No harm in that.'

'As long as you're not taken in.'

'I'm not. These days, nothing and nobody manages to deceive me.'

He raised his glass to her in an ironic salute.

'This is quite a coincidence,' he said. 'I wonder which of us is more shocked.'

'We'll never know.'

'Just now you were very determined to say we didn't know each other.'

'Would you have said differently?' she asked, watching him.

'No, but I doubt I'd have said it so fast or emphatically. You denied knowing me as though your life depended on it.'

'But we didn't know each other. Once we believed we did but we were both wrong. You thought I was easy to fool or you wouldn't have wasted your time on me. You never reckoned on Tania turning up and showing me what you were really like.'

'I admit I once had a relationship with Tania, but it was over.'

'Was it? I don't think she believed that. She still felt you were hers. That's why she felt so betrayed when she saw us. No, it was me you were planning to leave. That's why you kept hinting about something you wanted to tell me. You said it wasn't easy, but then it's never easy to dump someone, is it?'

He turned very pale. 'Isn't it? You dumped me without any trouble.'

'Dumping you was the easiest thing I'd ever done, but that's because you gave me cause.'

'But the way you did it—vanishing so that I could never find you. Can you imagine what I went through? It was like searching for a ghost. I nearly went mad because you denied me any chance to explain—'

'Explain what? That you were fooling around with both of us? If you'd been the man I thought you— Well, let's leave it there. You weren't that man and you never could be. It's best if we remain strangers now.'

'Remain?' he echoed sharply. But then his voice changed to wry, slightly bitter ac-

ceptance. 'Yes, we always were strangers, weren't we?'

'Always were, always will be. That's a very good business arrangement.'

'And you're a businesswoman?'

'Exactly. It's what I choose to be. *Capisci?*'

He nodded. '*Capisco.* I understand.'

'From now on, it's all business. The past didn't happen. It was an illusion.'

'An illusion—yes. I guessed that when you vanished into thin air. And now you've reappeared just as suddenly.'

'Another illusion. I'm not really here.'

'So if I look away you'll vanish again?'

'Perhaps that's what I ought to do.'

'No,' he said with a hint of suppressed violence. '*No!* Not again. You could never understand how I— Don't even think of it. *Capisci?*'

'*Capisco.* I understand very well.'

'Promise me that you won't leave.'

'All right.'

'On your word of honour.'

'Look—'

'Say it. Let me know that I can trust you this time at least.'

'Trust me *this time*? As though I was the one who deceived— You've got a nerve.'

'He's coming back,' Mario said hurriedly,

glancing to where Giorgio had appeared. 'Smile.'

She tried to look at ease but it was hard, and as soon as Giorgio reached the table she rose.

'I'm going to bed,' she said. 'It's been a long day for me, with the flight.'

'You're right; get some rest,' Mario said. 'We'll all meet here tomorrow morning at nine.'

They shook hands and she departed at once.

Giorgio watched her go, then eyed Mario wryly.

'What's going on with you two?' he queried. 'You're on edge with each other. For a moment I really thought there'd been something between you.'

'Not a thing,' Mario assured him. 'And there never could be.'

'Pity. Romeo and Juliet were "star-crossed lovers". It could have been interesting to have them promoted by another pair of star-crossed lovers. After all, if a couple is meant for each other but just can't get it together—well, it's not in their hands, is it? They just have to enjoy it while they can, but then accept that fate is against them.'

'Isn't that giving in too easily?'

'It's what Romeo and Juliet had to accept.'

'And then they died.'

'They died physically, but it doesn't usually happen that way. Sometimes people just die inside.'

'Yes,' Mario murmured. 'That's true.'

'I'll call the other members of the group and fix a meeting. They'll just love her. We've found the right person. Don't you agree?'

Mario nodded and spoke in an iron voice. 'The right person. Not a doubt of it. I must be going. My work has piled up while I've been away.'

He departed fast, urgently needing to get away from Giorgio's sharp eyes that saw too much for comfort.

Upstairs, he headed for his bedroom, but paused before entering. The room allocated to Natasha was just across the corridor and he went to stand outside, looking at her door, wondering what was happening behind it.

The evening had torn his nerves to shreds. The woman he'd met had been as unlike the sweet, charming girl he remembered as steel was unlike cream. His heart told him it was impossible that they should be the same person, but his brain groaned and said it was true.

This was the heartless creature who had

vanished without giving him a chance to defend himself, leaving him to hunt frantically for weeks until he'd realised that it was hopeless. And her manner towards him had left no doubt that she was enjoying her triumph.

A sensible man would have sent her away at once. Instead, he'd prevented her leaving, driven by instincts he didn't understand, nor want to face.

From behind her door came only silence. He moved closer, raising his hand to knock, then dropping it again. This wasn't the right moment.

Instead of going into his room, he turned away again and went downstairs into the garden, hoping some time in the night air would clear the confusion in his mind. But also doubting that anything would ever be clear again.

Natasha paced her room restlessly. After such a day she should have been ready to collapse into sleep, but her nerves were tense and she feared to lie awake all night, thinking the very thoughts she wanted to avoid.

Mario had blamed her for disappearing without giving him a chance to defend himself, and in so doing he'd touched a nerve.

Perhaps I should have let him say something, she thought. *Why didn't I?*

Because I'm my mother's daughter, said another voice in her mind. *And I can't help living by the lessons she taught me. Never trust a man. Don't believe his explanation because it'll be lies and you'll only suffer more. In fact, don't let him explain at all. Never, never give him a second chance.*

She'd fled Mario because she feared to listen to what he might have to say. Thinking the worst of him felt safer. That was the sad truth.

But now, meeting him again and getting a sense of his torment, she felt uneasy about her own actions.

'No,' she said. 'No, I'm not going down that road. What's done is done. It's over.'

In the last year she'd often suffered from insomnia and had resorted to some herbal sleeping pills. She took them out now, considering.

'I'm not lying awake fretting over him. This is war.'

She swallowed two pills but, instead of going to bed, she went outside for a few minutes. The tall window opened onto a balcony where she could stand and look down on a narrow strip of garden. There were flowers, a few trees and beyond them the Adige River, glowing in the evening light. Now it was easy to slip into the balcony scene and become Juliet, yearning over the man who'd captured her heart before she knew who he was. When she'd realised that she'd fallen in love with an enemy, it was too late.

'Too late,' she murmured. 'The last thing I wanted was to meet him again. I came here to start a new life. *Mario, Mario, wherefore art thou, Mario?* But it had to be you, didn't it? When I'm looking forward to meeting new people, you have to pop up. *Wherefore did thou do this, varlet?*'

In her agitation she said the words aloud. Alarmed at herself, she retreated through the window, shutting it firmly.

Outside, all was quiet. Darkness was falling, and there was nobody to notice Mario standing, alone and silent, beneath the trees. He had come straight into the garden after leaving Natasha's door, wondering if some light from her room would reassure him. What he had seen stunned and confused him. Her whispered words seemed to float down, reaching him so softly that he couldn't be sure he'd actually heard them.

To believe what he longed to believe was

something he refused to do. That way lay
danger, disillusion—the things he'd promised himself to avoid in future. So he backed
into the shadows, his eyes fixed on her window until the light went out and his world
was full of darkness.

Promptly at nine o'clock the next morning
Mario appeared at the breakfast table, frowning as he saw only Giorgio there.

'Where is she?' he demanded. 'I told her
nine o'clock.'

'Have a heart,' Giorgio begged. 'It's only a
few minutes after nine. She's not a machine,
just a lovely lady.'

'She is an employee being paid a high sal-
ary, for which I expect punctuality and obe-
dience to my wishes. Kindly call her room.'

'I've been calling it for half an hour,' Giorgio admitted. 'But there's no reply. Perhaps
she doesn't want to talk to us.'

Or perhaps she can't, said a voice in Mario's mind. He remembered the woman she
had been the evening before, bright, completely at ease, ready to challenge him every
moment.

Yet there had been something else, he realised. Beneath her confident manner he'd
sensed something different—troubled, un-

easy. Their meeting had taken them both by surprise. His own turmoil had startled and shaken him, making him struggle not to let her suspect his weakness, the more so because she had seemed free of any weakness.

But then he'd seen a new look in her eyes, a flash of vulnerability that matched his own. It had vanished at once, but for a brief moment he'd known that she was as alarmed as he was.

He remembered how he'd stood under her balcony last night, watching her, sensing again that she was haunted, but resisting the impulse to reach out to her. Her disappearance now hinted at new trouble. If he went to her room, what would he find? The confident Natasha, laughing at his discomfiture? Or the frail Natasha who couldn't cope?

Abruptly he took out his mobile phone, called her room and listened as the bell rang and rang, with no reply.

'If it was anyone else you'd think they'd vanished without paying the bill,' Giorgio observed. 'But we're not charging her for that room, so she's got no reason to vanish.'

'That's right,' Mario said grimly. 'No reason at all.'

'I'll go and knock on her door.'

'No, stay here. I'll see what's happened.'

Swiftly, he went to his office and opened a

cupboard that contained the hotel's replacement keys. Trying to stay calm despite his growing worry, Mario took the one that belonged to Natasha's room and went upstairs. After only a moment's hesitation, he opened her door.

At once he saw her, lying in bed, so still and silent that alarm rose in him. He rushed towards the bed and leaned down to her, close enough to see that she was breathing.

His relief was so great that he grasped the chest of drawers to stop himself falling. Every instinct of self-preservation warned him to get out quickly, before he was discovered. But he couldn't make himself leave her. Instead he dropped onto one knee, gazing at her closely. She lay without moving, her lovely hair splayed out on the pillow, her face soft and almost smiling.

How he had once dreamed of this, of awakening to find her beside him, sleeping gently, full of happiness at the pleasure they had shared.

He leaned a little closer, until he could feel her breath on his face. He knew he was taking a mad risk. A wise man would leave now, but he wasn't a wise man. He was a man torn by conflicting desires.

Then she moved, turning so that the bedclothes slipped away from her, revealing that she was naked. Mario drew a sharp breath.

How often in the past had he longed to see her this way? He had planned and schemed to draw her tenderly closer! The night of their disaster had been meant to end like this, lying together in his bed, with him discovering her hidden beauty. But then a calamity had descended on him and wrecked his life. How bitter was the irony that he should see her lovely nakedness now.

She moved again, reaching out in his direction, so that he had to jerk away quickly. She began to whisper in her sleep, but he couldn't make out the words. Only escape would save him. He rose, backed off quickly and managed to make it to the door before her eyes opened. Once outside, he leaned against the wall, his chest heaving, his brain whirling.

At last he moved away, back to the real world, where he was a man in command. And that, he vowed, was where he would stay.

Giorgio looked up as Mario approached. 'No luck finding her?'

Mario shrugged. 'I didn't bother looking very far. Try calling her again.'

Giorgio dialled the number, listening with a resigned face.

'Looks like she still isn't—no, wait! Natasha, is that you? Thank goodness! Where have you been? *What?* Don't you know the time? All right, I'll tell Mario. But hurry.' He shut off the phone. 'She says she overslept.'

Mario shrugged. 'Perhaps the flight tired her yesterday.'

Giorgio gave a rich chuckle. 'My guess is that she was entertaining someone last night. I know she'd only just arrived, but a girl as lovely as that can entertain anyone whenever she wants. I saw men looking at her as she came down those stairs. Did you expect such a beauty?'

'I didn't know what to expect,' Mario said in a toneless voice.

'Nor me. I never hoped she'd be so young and lovely. Let's make the best of it. Juliet come to life. Oh, yes, finding her was a real stroke of luck.'

A stroke of luck. The words clamoured in Mario's brain, adding more bitterness to what he was already suffering. He didn't believe that a man had been in Natasha's room last night, but the sight of her naked had devastated him. He could almost believe she'd done it on purpose to taunt him, but the sweet, enchanting Natasha he'd known would never do that.

But was she that Natasha any more?

Had she ever been?

'I just know what she's doing right this minute,' Giorgio said with relish. 'She's turning to the man next to her in the bed, saying, "You've got to go quickly so that nobody finds you here." Perhaps we should have someone watch her door to see who comes out.'

'That's enough,' Mario growled.

'With a girl as stunning as that, nothing is ever enough. Don't pretend you don't know what I mean. You were fizzing from the moment you saw her.'

'Drop it,' Mario growled.

'All right, you don't want to admit she had that effect on you. After all, you're the boss. Don't let her guess she's got you where she wants you—even if she has.'

I said drop it.

'Steady there. Don't get mad at me. I was only thinking that if there's an attraction between you, we can make use of it.'

'And you're mistaken. There's no attraction between us.'

'Pity. That could have been fun.'

Slowly, Natasha felt life returning to her as she ended the call from Giorgio.

'Nine-fifteen!' she gasped in horror. 'I

was supposed to be downstairs at nine. Oh, I should never have taken those sleeping pills.'

The pills had plunged her into a deep slumber, which she'd needed to silence her desperate thoughts of Mario. But at the end he'd invaded her sleep, his face close to hers, regarding her with an almost fierce intensity. But he wasn't there. It had been a dream.

'I just can't get away from him,' she whispered. 'Will I ever?'

She showered in cold water, relishing the feeling of coming back to life. Dressing was a simple matter of putting on tailored trousers and a smart blazer and fixing her hair back tightly. Then she was ready to go.

She found Giorgio and Mario downstairs at the table.

'I'm so sorry,' she said. 'I didn't mean to be late but I was more tired than I realised.'

'That's understandable,' Giorgio said gallantly.

Mario threw him a cynical look but said nothing.

'Where's that waiter?' Giorgio asked, frowning. 'I'll find him and he can bring you breakfast.'

He vanished.

'I'm glad Giorgio's gone,' she said. 'It gives us a chance to talk honestly. Last night you

stopped me getting out of my chair, and told
me to stay. But is that really what you want?
Wouldn't you be better off without me?'

'If I thought that I'd have said so,' he retorted.

'But think of it, day after day, trying not
to get annoyed with each other, pretending to
like each other. Surely you don't want that?
I'm giving you the chance to get rid of me,
Mario.'

'What about you? Do you want to make a
run for it?'

'I can cope.'

'But you think I can't. Thanks for the vote
of confidence. We're business professionals
and on that basis it can work.'

'You're right,' she said. 'Shake.'

'Shake.' He took her extended hand. 'Perhaps I should warn you that Giorgio has some
rather fancy ideas about you. He thinks you
had a lover in your room last night and that's
why you overslept.'

'*What?* I'd taken some herbal pills to get to
sleep after a strenuous day. A lover? I'd only
been here five minutes.'

'Giorgio sees you as the kind of woman
who can attract men as fast as that.'

'Cheek!'

'In his eyes it's a compliment.'

She scowled for a moment, then laughed. 'I guess I'll learn to put up with him.'

Giorgio reappeared with her breakfast.

'Eat up and we'll get to work,' he said. 'I'll get you a map of Verona.'

'I've got one,' she said, drawing it from her bag. 'I bought it at the airport so that I would be ready. The more you plan, the simpler life is.'

'True,' Mario murmured, 'but there are some things that can never be planned.'

'And you can't always anticipate what they might be,' she agreed. 'You can try, but—' She shrugged.

'But they always take you by surprise,' he murmured.

'Not always. Just sometimes. It's best to be ready.'

Giorgio looked from one to the other as if his alarm bells had sounded again.

'It's time we were making plans,' he said. 'I've called the others in the group, and they're dying to meet you. We're all invited to dinner tonight at the Albergo Splendido.' He beamed at Natasha. 'It'll be your big night.'

'Then I'd better prepare for it,' she said. 'I'll look around Verona today so that I can sound knowledgeable at the dinner. Otherwise they'll think I'm an amateur.'

'Good thinking,' Giorgio said. 'I'll escort you, and we'll have a great time.'

'Now, here—' Natasha pointed to a street on the map '—this is the Via Capello, where I can visit Juliet's house. I'd like to go there first, then the house where the Montagues lived. Finally, I'd like to see the tomb. Then I can work out my plans.'

'We'll leave as soon as you've finished breakfast,' Mario told her.

CHAPTER THREE

THE CHAUFFEUR-DRIVEN CAR was waiting for them, and soon they were on their way around the city.

Natasha already knew a good deal about Verona, having read about it on the plane. It was an old city, much of which went back to Roman times, two thousand years ago. Several places survived from that era, including a huge arena where gladiators had once slain their victims, but now was used for musical performances.

The streets were lined with historic buildings, many hinting at mystery and romance, all seeming to come from a more intriguing and beautiful age. She kept her eyes fixed on them as they drove through the town, trying to absorb its atmosphere.

'We're just turning into the Via Capello,' Mario said. 'We'll reach Juliet's house at any moment.'

A few minutes later the car dropped them at the entrance to a short tunnel. They joined the crowd walking through to the courtyard at the far end, where the balcony loomed overhead. Natasha regarded it with shining eyes.

'It's lovely,' she said. 'Of course I know it was put up less than a hundred years ago, but it looks right. It fits the house so perfectly that you can almost see Juliet standing there.'

'She's actually over there,' Giorgio said, pointing at a figure standing a little ahead, beneath and to the side of the balcony. It was a bronze statue of a young woman.

'Juliet,' she breathed.

As she watched, a woman walked up to the statue and brushed her hand against its breast. She was followed by another woman, and another, then a man.

'It's a tradition,' Mario explained. 'Everyone does it in the hope that it will bring them good luck. That's why that part of her is shining, because it's touched so often. People like to make contact with Juliet because they see her as a woman who knows more about love than anyone in the world.'

'Perhaps that's true,' Natasha murmured. 'But she knows tragedy as well as love.'

Intrigued, she went to stand before the statue. Juliet's head was turned slightly to the side, gazing into the distance as though only in another world could she find what she sought.

Natasha watched as a woman touched Juliet, closed her eyes and murmured something. At last her eyes opened and she stepped back with a smile, evidently feeling that she had received an answer.

If only it was that simple, Natasha thought. *If Juliet really could give me advice I'd ask her about the way my head is whirling, about how I'm feeling, and how I ought to be feeling. But she can't help me because she doesn't exist. She never really did, not the way people believe in her. That kind of love is just an illusion.*

She turned away to find Mario waiting. He moved closer, leaving Giorgio at a distance, and speaking quietly.

'Were you consulting Juliet?' he asked, raising an eyebrow.

'No,' she said. 'She's a fantasy. Nothing more.'

'How very prosaic.'

'I am prosaic, and I'm glad. It's useful.'

'But if you're going to promote the romantic fantasy, shouldn't you believe in it?'

She surveyed him with her head on one side and a faint ironic smile on her face.

'Not at all,' she said. 'It isn't necessary to believe something to persuade other people that it's true.'

'I wonder if you're right.'

A flash of anger made her say quickly, 'You know I'm right. We all know it at heart.'

'So—' he hesitated '—you're telling me that you've toughened up?'

'By a mile. So beware.'

'No need to tell me that.'

'So I've got you worried already? Good.'

For a wild moment he was tempted to tell her of the confused reactions that had rioted in him when he first saw her on the stairs. There had been an incredible moment of pleasure that the sight of her had always brought him, and which even now remained. But it had collided with a sense of alarm, as though a warning bell had sounded, letting him know that she would bring fear and darkness into his life.

But he suppressed the impulse to speak. How satisfied she would be to know that she could still throw him into confusion.

'Don't tell me I'm the only one who's toughened up,' she challenged him. 'Haven't you?'

'No doubt of it. It's called survival.'

She nodded. 'Right. As long as we both understand that, there's no problem.'

For them there would always be a problem. But there was no need of words.

'Now, I have a job to do,' she said briskly.

'Yes, let's look around further.'

Suddenly there was a cry from the far side of the courtyard.

'Buongiorno, amici!'

'Amadore!' Giorgio exclaimed, extending his hand in welcome.

The three men exchanged greetings in Italian, until Giorgio said, '*Signorina*, this is Amadore Finucci, a fellow member of the *Comunità*. Amadore, this is the Signorina Natasha Bates, who doesn't speak Italian.'

'Then it will be my pleasure to speak English,' Amadore said, seizing her hand.

She gave a polite response and he carried her hand to his mouth.

'Miss Bates,' he said.

'Please, call me Natasha.'

'Thank you—Natasha. When did you arrive?'

'Yesterday,' Giorgio said. 'Your father has invited us to dine at your hotel tonight.'

'Yes, he told me. I must leave now, but I look forward to seeing you this evening.'

He departed. Natasha eyed Mario curiously, puzzled to find him frowning.

'You're not pleased about this invitation?'

'That's because his hotel is one of the most luxurious in town,' Giorgio said. 'Mario's jealous.'

'I'm not jealous,' Mario said firmly. 'I admit I envy him having a bottomless pit of money to spend on the place.'

'His ballroom has to be seen to be believed,' Giorgio told her.

'Ballroom,' she echoed. 'Romeo and Juliet met in a ballroom.' She turned to Mario. 'Does your hotel have a ballroom?'

'No. None of the other hotels do.'

'Then that gives me an idea. Can we return to the hotel now? I need to get to work.'

'Aren't we going on to Romeo's house?' Giorgio asked.

'I'll do that tomorrow. Today, I have urgent things to do.

'Could you please provide me with a list of every member of the *Comunità*, and their hotels? Then I can check their locations and assess their requirements.'

'I'll see to it as soon as we arrive.'

As they walked back to the car, Giorgio murmured to Mario, 'A woman who knows her own mind. Perhaps we should beware.'

'There's no perhaps about it,' Mario replied grimly.

On the way back to the hotel Natasha took out her notebook and wrote in it swiftly and fiercely. Ideas were coming to her in cascades and she needed to capture them fast. This was the part of any project that she liked best. So absorbed did she become that she was unaware of the journey, and looked up suddenly when the car stopped.

'We're here,' Mario said. He'd been watching her silently.

'I need something to eat,' Giorgio declared. 'Suppose we meet downstairs in half an hour, for a feast?'

'Not me, thank you,' Natasha said. 'Perhaps you could send something up to my room?'

'But we could all celebrate together,' Giorgio protested.

'We can celebrate when I've made a success of this job. Let's hope that happens.'

'It'll happen,' Giorgio said. 'You're going to be just fantastic, isn't she, Mario?'

'No doubt of it,' he said bleakly.

'You're very kind, both of you. Now, excuse me, gentlemen.'

Giving them both a polite smile, she headed for the lift.

Upstairs, she plunged into work, making

more notes about the morning before things went out of her head. She was so immersed in her work that at first she didn't hear the knock on the door. It had to be repeated louder to capture her attention.

'Sorry,' she said, pulling it open, 'I got so—' She checked herself at the sight of Mario standing there with a trolley of food.

'Your meal, *signorina*,' he said.

She stared at the sight of the food. Someone had taken a lot of trouble preparing this meal, which Mario laid out for her with care.

'Giorgio told the kitchen to produce their best, to make sure you stay with us,' he said. 'So you have chicory risotto, followed by tiramisù, with Prosecco.'

Her favourite wine. How many times had he ordered it for her in Venice? And he had remembered.

'It's delicious,' she said politely as she ate.

'I'll tell Giorgio you approve. And I brought you this,' he said, handing her a large file.

It was the information she'd requested about the *Comunità*—hotels, owners, background information.

'That man I met today seems to come from the biggest and best,' she said, flicking through it. 'The Albergo Splendido.'

'It was a palace once. You'll like it. You're making a considerable impression, you know.'

'Amadore certainly seemed to think so.'

'Just don't take him too seriously. He flirts with every woman on the planet.'

She gave a brief laugh. 'You warned me about Giorgio; now you're warning me about Amadore. But you don't need to. I can recognise when a man is role-playing. He puts on a performance as the "romantic Italian" because he thinks an Englishwoman is bound to be fooled. I don't mind. He's charming. But don't expect me to fall for it.'

'I suppose I should have known you'd say that,' Mario growled. 'I wonder if you ever fall for anything.'

'Not these days. Never again.'

'And you think that's admirable?'

'I think it's safe.'

'And safety matters more than anything else? Never mind who you hurt.'

She turned on him, her quick temper rising. 'Who *I* hurt? Did I really hear you say that? After what you did?'

'I didn't do what you thought I did, and I could have explained. But you vanished without giving me a chance to defend myself.'

'What was there to defend? I know what I saw.'

'Natasha, why won't you realise that you misunderstood what you saw? Yes, I'd been having an affair with Tania. I'm not a saint. I've never pretended to be. But it was only a casual relationship and I'd started to feel that it must end. Things had changed in my life. I'd met you and nothing looked the same. I had to face the fact that I wanted you, not her.

'So that day I met Tania and told her we couldn't be together any more. But I couldn't make her believe it. When I left her she followed me, and that was how she found us together.

'I went after her, trying to explain that I was sorry to hurt her, but she screamed at me and ran off. I came back to our table, hoping I could make you understand. But you were gone. I tried your phone but you'd turned it off. I went to the hotel but you'd left just a few minutes earlier. Over the next few days I tried your phone, your email, your apartment, but you'd shut off every way of contacting you. It was like you'd ceased to exist.'

'Exactly. I *had* ceased to exist. The girl I was then—naive, slightly stupid, ready to be fooled—vanished into nothing. But now there's another woman in her place— suspicious, awkward, ready to give as good as she gets. She exists. She's me. She's rather hard. You won't like her. Be wise. Get rid of her.'

His face was suddenly tense. 'I think not. I prefer to keep her around and make her face up to what she did.'

'Is that why you got me back here?'

'What do you mean by that?'

'I don't believe it's coincidence that we just happened to meet again.'

He paled. 'You think I manipulated this situation?'

'You could have.'

'And I'm telling you I didn't. How dare you? Perhaps I should accuse *you* of manipulation. Did you persuade your friend to let you take her place?'

'No way. I had no idea you'd be here until I saw you on the stairs.'

'Nor I. Let's get this clear, Natasha. I didn't trick you into coming here. I didn't want to see you again, not after the way you behaved.'

'The way *I*—?'

'You left me feeling as though I was hanging off the edge of a cliff.'

'I know that feeling,' she said softly, with anger in her voice.

'All right. For the moment we have to accept things as they are. We're enemies but we need to be allies as far as this job's concerned. Our fight is still on, but it's a fair fight.'

'Is it? I wonder if your idea of a fair fight is the same as mine.'

'I guess we'll find that out.'

A beep from her mobile phone interrupted him. Answering it, she found a text:

You didn't have to run away. We can sort this out.

There was no name, but there didn't need to be. This wasn't the first text that Elroy Jenson had sent her since he'd shut her out of his media empire. Clearly he'd expected her to cave in and come crawling back.

She had to make him stop doing this.

Swiftly, she texted back:

Forget me, as I've forgotten you.

His reply came at once:

If that were true you wouldn't have run away. Come home. I can do a lot for you.

She groaned, wondering how much more of this she could take. She'd thought that by coming to Italy she could put Jenson behind her.

'What's the matter?' Mario asked. 'Who has upset you?'

'It's nothing,' she said quickly. 'I'm fine.'

'I don't think so. Perhaps you should change your mobile number. Doing that works well because then the guy can't reach you. But of course you know that. Here—'

Before she could stop him he'd seized the phone from her hand and was reading the text.

'Just tell him to— What does he mean, run away?'

'I've been running away from him for months. He's Elroy Jenson, the man who owns a great media empire. It stretches all over the world—England, America, Europe—'

'Yes—' Mario broke in '—I've heard of him. Some of his papers are in this country. Not a man you'd want to antagonise.'

'I used to make a good living writing for his newspapers and magazines, but then he decided that he fancied me. I didn't fancy him but he wouldn't take no for an answer. He kept pestering me until I slapped his face. Unfortunately, some of his employees saw it and the word got out. Since then none of his editors will buy articles from me.'

'And he keeps sending you these messages? Why don't you just change your mobile phone number?'

'I have. Several times. But he always manages to get the new one. He's a powerful man and his tentacles stretch far.'

'Bastardo!'

'If that means what I think it does, then yes. Now I can't earn a living in England and he's coming after me.'

'Thinking you'll turn to him for the money? And he'd like that—knowing that you'd only given in to him out of need?'

'He'd enjoy it. He's that kind of man. But he's going to be disappointed. I'll do anything rather than what he wants.'

'Anything? Including taking a job with a man you hate?'

'Even that. This job's a lucky break for me. It gets me out of England.'

'But you have to put up with me.'

'Stop being melodramatic. You're not so bad. I can manage. We've put the past behind us.'

He smiled wryly, trying to come to terms with her words. 'You're not so bad' implied a casual acceptance that should have been a relief but felt more like an insult.

'Yes, we've put it all behind us,' he agreed. 'And now we can concentrate on business, which is what we're here for. You need to make a living and I need to repay the bank loans I had to take out to buy this place.'

'That must be a heavy burden,' she said.

'It is. Damiano wanted to help me by lending me some money, and standing guarantor for the bank loan. But I wouldn't let him do either. This is my hotel, and mine alone.'

'I remember meeting Damiano in Venice. And his wife. They were very nice to me.'

'They both liked you a lot.'

In fact both Sally and Damiano had nudged him, saying, 'She's the one, Mario. Go on, make sure of her.'

And when things went wrong they had united again to call him 'The biggest idiot of all time'. It was a remark that still stung him.

'Why wouldn't you let him help you?' she asked.

'I just prefer to control my own life,' he said in a voice that was suddenly hard.

A tantalising memory flickered through her mind: Mario, two years ago, young, carefree and easy-going. Somehow he had changed into this grimly self-sufficient man who mistrusted the world.

'I prefer it too,' she said. 'You feel safer, like wearing a suit of armour. But is that always a good thing to wear?'

'That depends on who challenges you,' he said.

His eyes, fixed on her, left her in no doubt

of his message. Her presence was a challenge, one that he would fight off ruthlessly.

'But you wouldn't need a suit of armour against your older brother,' she said. 'Helping you is surely what older brothers are for?'

'Possibly, but I needed to stop being the younger brother, leaning on him. I told him I could do it alone, so I've got to prove that's true. I simply mustn't fail.'

'And I mustn't fail either,' she said, 'so in future we're going to concentrate on being practical. Please leave me now, and when I've finished my research I'll see you and Giorgio at supper.'

'Good luck with the work,' he said, and departed.

He went quickly to his office and went online. A few minutes' research told him all he needed to know about Elroy Jenson: his creation of a media empire, his money, his far-reaching power.

But it was the man's looks that amazed him. He'd expected a slobbering, middle-aged monster, a man no woman could want to be with unless she was after his money. But Jenson was well built, even handsome, with a riotous head of curly hair. A woman lucky enough to have captured his attention would have every reason to flaunt her triumph.

But not Natasha.

No man impresses her, he thought. *She decides what she wants, and woe betide him if he can't live up to it.*

He glanced at himself in the mirror.

'But could any man live up to it?' he murmured.

Researching the Albergo Splendido, Natasha could easily believe that it had started life as a palace. It was seven hundred years old and magnificently built.

To dine there meant dressing in style. Luckily she'd brought with her a black satin figure-hugging dress that managed to be both decorous and elegant.

Giorgio nodded approval. 'Lovely. You'll make their heads spin. Let's go.'

As they walked to the car Mario said, 'Aren't you making too much of her appearance? Surely it's her efficiency we need to promote?'

'Efficiency alone isn't enough. She's got that extra "something" special, and it's going to make all the difference.'

'I'll take your word for it,' Mario said coldly.

At the hotel Amadore was waiting for

them. 'Everyone's here,' he said. 'They're longing to meet you.'

He led her into a room filled with tables at which sat crowds of men and women, who broke into applause at the sight of her.

There could be no doubt that she was the star of the evening. Amadore introduced her to each guest, one by one, giving the name of the person and of their hotel.

'Ah, yes,' she said to one elderly man. 'That's the place where—'

He listened, open-mouthed, as she revealed her in-depth research. She did the same thing with several of the other hotel owners and was rewarded by looks of admiration.

'You see what I mean?' Giorgio murmured to Mario. 'A brilliant lady, clever and hard-working. We've struck gold.'

Mario didn't reply.

When she'd met all the guests she sat down at the head table for the meal, which turned out to be a glorious banquet, adorned with the finest wines.

'Mmm, lovely,' she said, sipping from her glass.

'Everyone thinks of Verona as the site of the love story,' Giorgio told her. 'But it's also surrounded by vineyards. Most of the hotel owners have some sort of investment in vine-yards.'

'The wine you're drinking now was pro-duced in my own vineyard,' Amadore said.

'It's delicious,' she said, sipping again.

'Thank you, *signorina*.'

They clinked glasses.

Soon she saw that everyone was looking at her expectantly.

'They're waiting for your speech,' Mario murmured.

'But I can only speak English,' she pro-tested. 'Will they understand?'

'Hotel owners tend to speak English be-cause your country sends us many tourists.'

Mario got to his feet.

'My friends,' he said, 'it has been our plea-sure tonight to meet the lady we've employed to promote us to the world. Now let us hear her plans.'

There was applause as Natasha rose. For a few moments she was nervous but the warm, friendly atmosphere enveloped her and she began to enjoy herself as she laid out the ideas that had been forming in her mind.

'Every hotel has something to connect it to the story,' she said. 'Some are near Juliet's house, some near Romeo's house, some are near the tomb.'

'Some of us aren't so lucky,' a man called. 'Our hotels aren't near anywhere significant.'

'Don't be so sure,' she said. 'Remember the scene where Romeo's friend Mercutio is stabbed to death by Juliet's kinsman? That happens outdoors in the street. But which street? Nobody knows for sure, but perhaps some of your hotels are nearby.'

Natasha looked out at her audience, smiling and nodding appreciatively as she spoke. She was fulfilling all their highest expectations. Applause rang in her ears.

CHAPTER FOUR

'NOW FOR THE next stage,' Natasha said. 'I'll want to talk to you all individually, and then I'm going to write my first piece explaining how "Romeo and Juliet" are still alive in Verona if people know how to find them. We'll invite them to come here, and stay in your hotels. By that time I'll have produced several more texts.'

'But who will publish these?' called a voice from the floor.

'Anyone she sends it to,' Giorgio called back. 'This lady is a very notable journalist with many connections. She gets published everywhere.'

More applause, but Natasha held up her hand for silence.

'We're not going to take chances,' she said. 'This "article" will actually be an advertisement. We buy a double-page spread and insert our own text and pictures. That way we can be sure of being read. What matters is to get things done the way we want. Of course it will be costly. Advertisements have to be paid for, and perhaps some of you won't want to accept that expense. Let's take a vote. Hands up anyone who's against the idea.'

Not a single hand was raised.

'We'll do it your way,' called a voice.

There were cheers and applause, which went on until they were interrupted by the sound of music.

'That's coming from the ballroom,' Amadore told her. 'Our guests like to dance in the evening.'

'A ballroom is wonderful,' she said. 'The Capulets gave a ball for Juliet and Paris, the man they wanted her to marry, which Romeo gatecrashed to see another girl that he was in love with. Instead he met Juliet and they fell in love within a few minutes. Without that ball it might never have happened.'

'Then come and have a look,' Amadore said eagerly.

Everyone crowded after them as he led her along a short corridor, throwing open a double door at the end, revealing a huge, beautiful room where couples were whirling.

'Perfect,' she murmured.

Amadore took her hand. 'Dance with me.'

Smiling, she let him draw her into his arms and guide her onto the floor. He was an excellent dancer and she responded gladly. When the music stopped another man stepped in to claim her, then another.

At last she found herself facing Mario.

'You've danced with everyone else,' he observed. 'Will it ever be my turn?'

'Not until you ask me.'

'No,' he said. 'I'm not going to ask you.'

But as he spoke his arm went around her waist in a grip too firm for her to resist, even if she had wanted to.

They had danced together once before. One night in Venice, when they had been having supper at an outdoor café in St Mark's Square, a band had started to play and before she knew it she was waltzing in his arms.

'Is this all right?' he'd whispered.

'I'll let you know later,' she had teased.

It had lasted only a few minutes, and she had promised herself that one day she would dance with him again. But the next day they had broken up, and it had never happened again. Until now.

It was unnerving to feel his arms around her, his hand on her waist, holding her close. Her heart was beating softly but fervently. She glanced at him, trying to know if he felt the same. Would he invite her to dance with him again?

But before he could speak they became aware of a middle-aged man on the edge of the crowd, trying to attract their attention.

'Ah, there's Francesco,' Mario said. 'I hoped he'd be here. He owns one of the biggest hotels, and I always like to have him on my side. Let's go and say hello.'

Francesco beamed, greeting Natasha with an embrace.

'It's a pleasure to meet you,' he said warmly. 'Now, let me introduce my daughter, Laura.'

The young woman with him was in her mid-twenties with a beautiful face and an air of confidence that came from being always in demand.

'How have you done?' she said carefully to Natasha.

'No,' her father interrupted her. 'Not like that, *cara*. The English say "How do you do?" not "How have you done?"'

'How do you do?' Laura echoed, smiling. 'Is that right?'

'That is perfect,' her father said.

He spoke proudly and Natasha knew a slight twinge of sadness as a memory came back to her from long ago. She had heard that pride before, in her own father's voice, in her childhood, before he'd abandoned her without a backward glance.

But this was no time to be brooding over the past. She thrust the memory aside, returning Laura's greeting with the appearance of warmth.

Then Laura turned her attention to Mario, saying, 'And how do you do?'

'There's no need for such formality,' Mario said, shaking her hand. 'We already know each other.'

'Indeed we do,' Laura said, glancing at Natasha as she spoke.

Natasha returned her look with interest. She had the feeling that Laura was sizing her up as possible competition.

Then Amadore appeared beside them. 'Do I get another dance?' he asked.

'Of course.' Natasha let the charming hotel owner enfold her in his arms and twirl her gently across the floor.

Out of the corner of her eye she could just see Mario gliding past with Laura, who seemed to be trying to dance as close to him as possible.

'There the women go again,' Amadore said, 'parading themselves to get his attention.'

'Do you mean Signor Ferrone?' Natasha asked.

'Oh, yes. He's a lucky man. Every female makes eyes at him, and the rumour is that he can have any woman he wants.'

So nothing had changed, she thought, remembering how women's eyes had followed Mario during their time together. How they had envied her, being with him. How little they had known how he could make a woman suffer.

'Look at that,' Amadore said, still regarding Mario with envy. 'The way she's pressed up against him is almost indecent.'

Natasha managed to chuckle. 'Oh, come on. A man's entitled to enjoy himself if he can.'

'That's very generous of you. Most women don't take such a relaxed view.'

'I can afford to be relaxed. My life is arranged just the way I want it.'

'You're luckier than most of us then.'

Mario, just a few feet away, glanced at them only briefly before swinging Laura away to the far side of the ballroom. There, he found more female attention to distract him from sights he didn't want to see and thoughts he didn't want to think.

But it lasted only a short time. When he next looked at Natasha she was sitting down scribbling in her notebook. Two men were sitting beside her, while another two looked over her shoulders. As the music came to an end he began to approach her, but Amadore detained him.

'Lovely lady,' he said. 'Every man is interested. Luckily she's not interested in them.'

'She told you that?'

'We were watching Laura making a play for you. I disapproved but she said you were entitled to enjoy yourself. I complimented her on her relaxed attitude and she said she could afford to be relaxed as her life was arranged the way she wanted it.'

'She probably just said that to shut you up.'

'Maybe. But it wouldn't surprise me if back home she has a trail of eager pursuers.'

'You could be right,' Mario growled.

He could see that Natasha had finished making notes, and was rising to move away. He got to her quickly.

'Still working?' he said.

'I've had an idea. I need to talk to everyone again.'

'Then let's return to the dining room.' He offered her his arm, saying, 'You've done well tonight. The contract will be ready soon.'

'Contract?'

'For you to sign. The whole *Comunità* is

determined to secure your professional services. Are you willing to stay with us?'

'Yes,' she said softly. 'I'm willing.'

When they were gathered in the dining room again she addressed everyone. 'I think we should take some photographs of Romeo and Juliet. They say a picture's worth a thousand words, and we can send ours all over the world. We'll need to hire actors, then we'll photograph them on the balcony, in the tomb, anywhere that seems atmospheric.'

'We can't pose them on the official balcony,' Mario said. 'There are always tourists there. But this hotel has a balcony that will do.'

It was agreed that they would all meet again when the arrangements were made. Now all Mario wanted was to get away. Nothing had prepared him for being so close to her for hours, and he needed to be alone.

'Sleep well,' he told her as he escorted her to a chauffeur-driven car. 'You've worked hard today and there'll be more tomorrow.' He opened the car door. 'I'll see you tomorrow morning. Goodnight.'

He walked away.

Back in her room, Natasha undressed and went to bed. It had been a successful evening and she should have felt triumphant. Perhaps she would have done if Mario had returned with her, and been here to share her sense of achievement. But he had left her alone while he spent the night somewhere else.

Images of Laura danced through her mind, pursued by Amadore's voice saying '…he can have any woman he wants.'

She tried to shut the thoughts down. She and Mario were no longer part of each other's lives, and she cared nothing where he was now, or who he was with.

She lay down and managed to sleep. When she awoke she could hear a noise in the corridor outside, as though someone was turning a key in a lock. She rose and opened her door just in time to see Mario's door closing.

It was six in the morning.

She half expected him to be late for breakfast but he was there before her, calm, collected and ready for work.

'You were right about hiring actors,' he said. 'We'll have a file of pictures soon. In the meantime I've been making some notes of my own—'

But before she could look at them her phone beeped with another text.

'Is he hounding you again?' Mario demanded.

'No, it's not him,' she said, looking at the screen. Then she drew in her breath sharply. 'Oh, no—no! *Please, no!*'

'What is it?'

'Nothing,' she said sharply.

'Don't tell me it's nothing when it affects you like that. Let me see.'

Without asking her permission, he took the phone from her.

'What's this?' he demanded, reading, *'Sorry, your cheque bounced.'*

'How dare you?' she said furiously, snatching the phone back.

'Who's hounding you for money? Is it him?'

'No, it's my friend Helen, and she's not hounding me. She's been letting me stay in her flat and she got me this job. Before I left I gave her a cheque for my share of expenses. I owe her so much and I've repaid her like this. I didn't mean to. I thought there was just enough in the bank.'

'Right, we'd better get your contract sorted at once. Wait for me here.'

As he left she sat there, deep in gloom. Shame pervaded her and for a moment she wished she could do what Mario had accused her of, and vanish into thin air.

After a few minutes Giorgio appeared.

'The boss says I'm to give you the contract to sign,' he told her. 'Let's go into his office.'

In the office he laid out papers before her. 'Just sign at the bottom.'

She picked up the pen, then paused. 'Wait, are you sure this contract is right?'

'The boss says it is.'

'But I know what the agency offered me— the money was far less.'

'The fee has been changed. The boss says you're worth more.'

Her head was spinning. The new amount was much larger than the one she had been quoted before.

'You need to give me your bank details so that some money can be paid to you today,' Giorgio said.

Dazed, she gave him the necessary information and signed the contract at the bottom of the last page.

'And you must put your initials on the other pages,' Giorgio told her. 'He wants to make very sure that you're ours and nobody else's. He knows good value when he sees it. Ah, here he is.'

Mario had come into the room, and stood watching as Natasha finished signing. Glancing over the papers, he nodded and handed them to Giorgio, who left the room.

'I hadn't expected so much,' she said. 'You didn't have to do that. But thank you.'

'You have nothing to thank me for, *signorina*,' he said firmly. 'You're vital to this project and I've taken the necessary steps to make sure the *Comunità* keeps your services.'

She nodded, replying in the same formal voice, 'You can be sure that I will remain loyal to the *Comunità, signore*.'

'Excellent,' he said. 'Then we understand each other.'

'I'm sure we do.'

Oh, yes, she thought. They understood each other perfectly, but in ways that could never be expressed in words. He'd moved swiftly to save her from disaster, but in such a way that there was no fear of them growing closer. They were *signore* and *signorina*, and nothing else.

Not long after, she accessed her bank account on the Internet and found that a large sum of money had already been deposited, enabling her to pay her debt to Helen. That was a relief and she was able to enjoy an hour wandering the streets, absorbing the feel of the city.

When she returned she found that the photographs had arrived. Giorgio and Mario were going through them, studying the pictures of young models, seeking one with the perfect combination of beauty and innocence. She joined in and after a while she discovered exactly what she wanted.

Finding Romeo was harder. He had to be handsome, with splendid legs, since Romeo would be wearing tights. At last she found what she wanted.

'Perfect,' Mario said, studying the picture. 'Good-looking and vulnerable.'

'Vulnerable?' Giorgio queried. 'He's one of literature's great heroes.'

'He also fell for everything that was said to him,' Mario observed wryly. 'Not one of the world's great minds.'

'That's what happens to people in love,' Natasha said. 'They set their minds aside and believe what they want to believe.'

'And soon learn their mistake. All right, let's hire these two.'

Giorgio got straight onto the phone, made the contact and arranged for the two young people to appear in a couple of days.

'Paolo and Lucia,' he said. 'They'll be here ready to start on Thursday morning.'

'That's fine,' Natasha said. 'It gives me some more time to work on my ideas.'

The next two days were abuzz with action. Some of the time was spent visiting Romeo's house, and twice Natasha was invited to dine with other members of the *Comunità*. Mario accompanied her on these trips, but did not sit next to her at the dinner table.

She thought she understood. Having tied her down with the contract, both legally and financially, Mario preferred to keep a certain distance between them.

But the money in her bank account was a big relief. There was no doubt that in Mario she'd made a good professional association. She must cling to that thought.

By day they were absorbed in preparing for the photo shoot. Giorgio hired a photographer experienced in taking dramatic pictures. He also found a theatrical costumier.

'She'll join us tomorrow with a big variety of costumes,' he told Natasha. 'Our models can try several until we find the right ones.'

'Juliet will need something exotic for the ballroom,' Natasha said. 'Then an elegant dress for the wedding scene, and a very simple one for the tomb. Right, I'm going to bed. It's going to be a busy day tomorrow.'

'Does anyone know where Mario is?' Giorgio enquired.

'He left an hour ago,' Natasha said. 'He must be busy.'

On the way upstairs she wondered if Mario

was in his room, or had he gone to be with the same person he'd probably visited the other night?

Passing his door, she couldn't help pausing to hear if any sound was coming from inside. She blamed herself for yielding to the temptation, but she couldn't help it.

Then she heard his voice. He was on the telephone, speaking Italian in a warm, laughing tone.

'Non è importante. Non è importante.'

She didn't need to know the language to understand what he was saying: 'It's not important'. Mario was reassuring somebody that what was happening now didn't matter to him.

She hurried into her room and locked the door, wishing she'd resisted temptation and vowing to be stronger next time.

Next morning Lisa, the costumier, arrived early. She was a tall businesslike woman who spoke perfect English and went through Natasha's requirements with no trouble.

'Let's hope Romeo is handsome and has a good figure,' she said briskly.

'He looked good in the photo I saw, but I haven't met him yet,' Natasha admitted.

'That's a pity. To be suitable he must be

sexy. We need the women to sigh over him and say, "I want some of that".'

'But he'll only be a picture,' Natasha protested. 'We're selling the town, not Romeo himself.'

Lisa chuckled. 'You think that, do you?'

Natasha gave a wry smile. 'Well, it's what I need to believe. But I guess you're right.'

'Share the joke, ladies,' Giorgio called from nearby, where he was talking with Mario.

'You wouldn't understand it,' Lisa told him. 'We're laughing at men, and men never realise how funny they are.'

'That's very true,' Natasha said. 'And if you try to explain they still don't understand.'

Mario gave her an odd glance which she returned with an air of teasing confidence. She felt a certain cheeky pleasure in having disconcerted him. The day had started well. Whatever happened now, she felt she could cope.

They all set out for the Splendido, where everyone was waiting, eager to begin. The next hour was spent going through a variety of garments.

'I like this one,' Natasha said, holding up a long white ballgown. It was simple and elegant, perfect for a girl making her debut in society. 'Juliet can wear this at the ball.'

Giorgio looked impatiently at his watch.

'They should be here by now. What's happened to them?'

He snatched up his phone and dialled. Almost as soon as he was through, an expression of outrage overtook him.

'Sì? Che cosa? Cosa vuol dire che non posso venire? Oh, dolore bene!'

He hung up.

'What's happened?' Mario demanded.

'They're not coming. There's been a mix-up with the dates. They thought the shoot was next week.'

'Oh, no, what are we going to do?' Natasha cried. 'It's all set up for today.'

'There's only one thing we can do,' Giorgio said. 'Find another Romeo and Juliet.'

'But we haven't got time to search,' she protested.

'We don't have to search. We've got the duo we need right here.' He threw out his arms towards her and Mario. 'Romeo and Juliet.'

She stared. 'You can't possibly be serious.'

'I'm perfectly serious. You're beautiful enough to be Juliet, and Mario can just about get by as Romeo.'

'It won't work,' Mario growled. 'As though I could—'

'It's got to work,' Giorgio said. 'You're the

only two who can do it in the time available. We've got to start right now, otherwise all our plans are in a mess. Come along, you two. Be professional.'

'He's right,' Mario growled. 'We have no choice.'

'Go next door and get changed,' Amadore said. 'Natasha, a maid will come with you.'

She looked around wildly. Surely there must be some other way. But there was no other way. Only this could save her plans for the success she simply had to have.

The maid appeared and took her to the room assigned as Juliet's dressing room. The dress fitted perfectly onto her slender, delicate figure. But her hair didn't seem right, pulled tightly back.

'I think Juliet would wear it hung loose,' she said.

The maid nodded, and got skilfully to work. Natasha watched, only half believing, as the self she knew disappeared and naive, vulnerable Juliet took her place. The merest touch of make-up heightened the impression, and she was ready to go.

As she entered the ballroom heads turned. Giorgio made a clapping movement and Amadore whistled.

She noticed neither of them. Her attention had been seized by the man standing a little further off. Mario had transformed into Romeo, wearing a dark blue doublet and tights. It would need a fine figure to get away with such a revealing costume, but Mario was tall, splendidly built and handsome enough to steal the spotlight.

Suddenly a memory came flooding back to her. Two years ago, during their precious short time together in Venice, they had spent a day on the beach. Her first sight of him, half naked in swimming trunks, had had a stunning effect on her, making her intensely aware that her own swimwear was a bikini, leaving much of her body uncovered.

Oh, yes, she'd thought as she enjoyed the sight of his long, strong legs as he raced across the beach. *Oh, yes!*

After that everything had changed. They spent the day chasing each other, bathing in the sea or stretched out on the sand, and with every moment she wanted him more. She'd feasted her eyes on his smooth, muscular body, seizing every chance to lean closer to him, cherishing the brief moments when her flesh brushed against his.

It had been her first experience of fierce desire and it revealed her to herself in a new light. In the past she had flirted, laughed, teased, but never before had she wanted a man with such fervour. When their eyes met she believed she saw the same intensity in him, and promised herself that soon he would carry her to a new world.

That night they'd parted with only a kiss. She had told herself he was biding his time, waiting for her to be ready to move on.

Three days later they had parted for ever.

Shaking off the memory, she began to walk towards Mario, tense for the moment when she would see his reaction to her. Would the past return to haunt him too? What would she see in his eyes?

At last Mario looked up, saw her and nodded.

'Splendid,' he said. 'Giorgio chose Juliet well.'

His tone was polite but nothing more, and his eyes were blank.

'And you look fine as well, Signor Ferrone,' she said, striving to match him for blandness.

'Well, like Giorgio said, I'll "just about get by".'

'Everybody ready?' Amadore called. 'This way.'

He indicated an archway at the far end of the ballroom. Mario offered Natasha his arm and she took it, saying, 'Thank you, *signore*.'

He leaned closer to her, murmuring, 'Don't call me *signore*. My name is Mario. If you address me formally people will think something is wrong between us.'

'And we mustn't let them think that,' she agreed. 'Shall we go?'

CHAPTER FIVE

THERE WAS A cheer when they came into the ballroom. Lisa nodded, as though to say that Romeo's looks met her high standards.

The photographer studied them with approval and said he would start with portrait shots.

'First I'll take you separately, then together. Juliet, you first.'

'Juliet? I'm Natasha,' she said lightly.

'No, today you are Juliet.'

'He's right,' Giorgio said. 'You don't pretend to be Juliet. You *are* Juliet. You can go back to being Natasha tomorrow.'

'If I want to,' she said, entering into the spirit. 'Natasha might be too boring.'

'That's the spirit,' Giorgio said with a grin.

She turned this way and that, smiled, looked sad, smiled again.

'Now throw your arms out,' Giorgio said. 'Imagine you're looking at someone who's the great happiness of your life.'

She did so, reaching towards the camera with a yearning look.

Mario, watching from the sidelines, turned his head to avoid seeing that expression on her face. He remembered it too well from the past, and couldn't bear to be reminded of it now that the past was over.

Then he too had to pose for portrait shots.

'This way, that way,' the photographer called. 'Turn your head a little. Good. Now the two of you together.'

The first shot was a formal pose, with Juliet standing just in front of Romeo, his hands on her shoulders.

'Now turn and look into each other's eyes. Keep hold of each other but lean back a little so that I can see both of your faces.'

They obeyed, studying each other seriously, then smiling according to instructions.

'I think Romeo should frown a little,' Lisa called. 'And he should try to look sexy so that we know why Juliet fell for him.'

Mario scowled, annoyed at the comment and even more exasperated by the fact that Natasha collapsed with laughter.

'Don't worry,' she called. 'I can pretend if I have to.'

'And perhaps Juliet had to,' Giorgio said cheerfully. 'Maybe she didn't really fancy

Romeo at all. She was pursuing her own agenda. *That's it!* Romeo, that grim look is perfect. Keep it up.'

'Yes, keep it up,' she chuckled. 'Just think how I'm going to thump you later.'

'Juliet, that smile is wonderful,' the photographer called. 'It says a lot about the kind of marriage they would have had if they'd lived. One where he got worked up and she laughed at him. I'm beginning to think nobody ever really understands this pair.'

'No,' she murmured so that only Mario could hear. 'Nobody really understands.'

'He's talking nonsense,' Mario growled.

'He's grandstanding to make us play our parts,' she said. 'It's his job. So we have to do ours.'

'Juliet,' Giorgio called, 'reach up and brush his hair forward a little, around his face.' She did so, hearing the camera click madly.

'That's it—now again—and again—gently—Juliet's longing to caress his face, and this is her chance.'

Natasha told herself that she was merely obeying orders, but she couldn't hide the truth from herself. She wanted to do this—wanted to touch his face, his body, his heart. Even through the lightness of her caress she felt the tremor that went through Mario, despite his attempt to suppress it. She could sense his reaction because it mirrored her own.

But could he suspect the feelings that were going through her at being so close to him? Suddenly, his face had softened. The grim look she saw on it so often faded, leaving a faint echo of the young, gentle man she had loved. His eyes were fixed on her intently but that might be no more than playing his part. If only she could tell.

'Right, that's it,' came Giorgio's voice. 'Now for the balcony scene. Come this way.'

The balcony at the back of the Splendido was decorated much like the one at Juliet's house, and had the advantage of being several feet lower so that Romeo and Juliet could be closer to each other. Mario stood below, reaching up, while Natasha leaned down to touch his hand while the camera clicked away.

'Perfect,' Giorgio cried at last. 'You two are doing a great job. It's wonderful how well you work together.'

They said what was necessary and followed him back to the ballroom, where another selection of garments was laid out for them.

'Romeo believes that Juliet is dead,' Giorgio said. 'So he comes to the crypt where her body lies. He finds her there, says his farewells and takes his own life. Then she wakes, finds him dead, and she too chooses death. We'll shoot this scene in the cellar.'

With the maid's help, Natasha donned a plain gown and they all went down to the hotel's cellar, where a stone bench had been prepared for her to lie on.

'Ow!' she said, stretching out on it. 'That stone's really hard.'

'Is it really painful?' Mario asked her quietly.

'No, I'll be all right.'

'Let me put something under your head.'

'No, that would spoil it. But thank you.'

He still looked worried but let it drop.

'Walk up to her body,' Giorgio said. 'Look into her face as though you can't believe it's true. Good. Just like that.'

Lying there with her eyes closed, Natasha yearned to open them and see Mario's expression, to meet his eyes. But she must resist temptation and be content with the feel of his breath on her face.

'Lay your head on her breast,' Giorgio instructed.

The next moment she felt him lying against her and gave a slight gasp.

'Now kiss her,' Giorgio said,

She braced herself for the moment his

mouth touched hers. It was the faintest possible sensation but she told herself to endure it.

'Again,' Giorgio said. 'Remember, you've lost the only woman in life that you could ever care about.'

Mario kissed her again before laying his head once more on her breast. At last Giorgio called out that the scene was over.

'Now for the big one,' he said. 'The moment when they meet.'

In the ballroom Natasha donned the glamorous gown and watched while the maid worked on her hair. When everything was ready Giorgio guided 'Romeo and Juliet' into position.

'It's during the ball. Juliet is standing there, watching everyone, particularly Paris, the man her parents want her to marry. But then she sees Romeo watching her. Their eyes meet.'

Mario turned his head so that he gazed at Natasha. She gazed back.

'He advances towards her,' Giorgio continued. 'That's right, Mario, a little nearer. He takes her hand, and asks forgiveness for touching her because he says he isn't worthy. But she says he is.'

Now Natasha's hand was clasped in Mario's. He was close to her, watching her intently.

'And Romeo dares to steal a kiss,' Giorgio said triumphantly. 'Go on. Let's catch that on camera.'

Gently Mario dropped his head, laying his lips on hers.

'Good,' Giorgio said. 'But I wonder if we should do it again. Natasha, it might be more effective if you put your arm around him.'

'It's too soon for that,' she said quickly. 'She doesn't yet know how she feels.'

'Nor does he,' Mario said. 'How would Romeo kiss her at this point? Would it be like this?' He laid his lips briefly over Natasha's. 'He might do it respectfully because however much he desires her he fears to offend her. Or is he a shameless character who simply takes what he wants, like this?'

His arm went around her waist, drawing her against him, while his mouth covered hers firmly and purposefully.

She was stunned. The brief, light kiss he'd given her a few moments ago hadn't prepared her for this. Instinctively, her hands moved to touch him, but she snatched them back, unsure whether she would embrace him or push him away. She understood nothing except the disturbing pleasure of his lips on hers, and the maddening instinct to slap his face.

For two years she'd wanted to be in his

arms, dreamed of it while mentally rejecting
it in her rage at his betrayal. Now the sweet-
ness of holding him again struggled with fury
at his assumption that he could do as he liked
and she would have to accept it.

But she could not repulse him. Whatever
common sense might dictate, she must appear to react to him blissfully and chance
what the future might bring. She let herself
press against him, eager to feel his response,
and then—

'All right, Giorgio?' Mario cried, standing
back. 'Is that what you want?'

Natasha froze, barely able to believe what
had happened. It seemed that the feelings that
had pervaded her had been hers alone. Had
he felt anything beyond the need to get the
photographs right? Fury simmered inside her.

'That's fine,' Giorgio said. 'Do it just like
that, for the camera.'

Then Mario's hands were on her again,
drawing her nearer so that he could lay his
lips on hers and hold her against him, unmov-
ing. She could feel the warmth of his mouth,
of his whole body, and her own responded to
the sensation whether she wanted it to or not.
Her anger flared further.

Somewhere in the background she could
hear the sound of a camera, clicking again

and again until at last Giorgio called, 'All right, that's it. Well done, you two. Now let's think about the next scene.'

'I need a little fresh air first,' Natasha said, quickly slipping out of the nearest door into a corridor.

She ran until she reached a corner behind which she could hide. She must escape Mario lest he suspect that she'd just discovered the power he still had over her.

But when she looked around she found him facing her.

'Did you follow me?' she demanded.

'I thought that was what you meant me to do. Don't you have something you want to say to me?'

'Oh, yes, I have a thousand things,' she said furiously. 'You've got a nerve, doing what you did back there.'

'Kissing you, you mean? But you owed it to me. When we parted you never kissed me goodbye.'

'I never thumped the living daylights out of you either, which I was surely tempted to.'

He seemed to consider this. 'So you think I deserve to have you slap my face? Very well. Do your worst.'

'What are you saying?'

'Go ahead. Slap me if it will make you feel better.'

He jutted his chin out a little and stood waiting.

'Stop talking nonsense,' she snapped.

'I mean it. You can do what you like and I promise not to retaliate.'

'This is all a big joke to you, isn't it?'

He shook his head. 'My sense of humour died the day you left. In the weeks I spent trying to find you I buried it deep underground. So what now? Aren't you going to hit me?'

'Certainly not. It would be unprofessional. I might leave marks on your face that would spoil the next photographs. The matter is closed.'

He saluted. 'Yes, ma'am. Whatever you say, ma'am.'

'Oh, stop it—stop it! Stop trying to make a fool of me, of yourself, of both of us.'

Suddenly, his manner changed. The wry irony died and a bleakness came into his eyes. 'You silly woman,' he said quietly. 'Don't you realise that we all have our own way of coping.'

'And that's your way? Well, this is my way.'

Without warning, the swift temper she'd vowed to control swept over her, driving her to do something she knew was madness. She seized his head in her hands, drew it down and covered his mouth with her own. At once she could feel his hands on her and sensed the same confusion as she had felt herself—to deny the kiss or indulge it joyfully?

But he was going to indulge it. That was her decision, and she would give him no choice. She slightly softened the pressure of her mouth so that the kiss could become a caress, her lips moving over his in a way she had once known delighted him. She sensed his response in his tension, the sudden tightening of his arms about her.

Now she was ready to taunt him further. The pressure of her mouth intensified, and his breath came faster as his excitement grew. His lips parted as he explored her more deeply. He was no longer merely receiving her kiss but returning it in full, seeking to take command but not succeeding. The command was hers, and she would keep it whether he liked it or not. Her spirit soared. She was winning.

He drew back a little. 'Natasha—'

'Take warning, Mario. Two can play this game. You won't defy me again. If you do I'll make you sorry.'

She felt him tense, saw his eyes full of disbelief as he understood her meaning. Then it was all over. 'You had to do that, didn't you?'

he rasped. 'You had to tease me—make me think—but it wasn't a kiss. It was revenge.'

'Revenge can be very sweet,' she said, pushing him away. 'That's one of the things I learned from you. Did you think you were going to get away with what you did back there? You just had to show me that you were the boss, and how I felt didn't count.'

He shook his head. 'You won't believe this,' he said in a hard voice, 'but I kissed you because I wanted to. I'm ashamed of that now because it seems so stupid to imagine that you had any kindly feelings left. But, idiot that I was, I thought some part of you might still be the old Natasha, the sweet-natured girl I loved and wanted to be with.

'But you warned me about that, didn't you? You told me that Natasha was dead. I couldn't believe it, but I believe it now. You did this to get your own back by reminding me of what I've lost.'

'You lost it because you didn't want it,' she said.

'Keep telling yourself that,' he said quietly. 'In the end you may come to believe it. In those days I wanted you more than I've ever wanted any woman. And I could have told you that if you hadn't vanished when you did. You landed us in this desert, not me. You did it by losing your temper and acting without thinking anything through. We didn't have to end up here. We could have been married by now, and expecting our first child. Instead— well, look at us.'

'Stop it! *Stop it!*' she screamed, turning away from him with her hands over her ears.

'Yes, the truth can be very painful, can't it? I could have devoted my life to loving you. Instead, I've come so close to hating you that it scares me.'

'Well, at least that's getting the truth out into the open. You hate me.'

'I didn't say that. I said I came close to hating you. I've never been able to take the final step, but I have a feeling that will come soon.'

She made no reply. The unexpected glimpse he'd given her of his own feelings had set off an aching misery inside her. He didn't hate her, but he would if he could. She wanted to scream and bang her head against the wall.

She turned away but he pulled her around to face him.

'You won't let me tell you my side of it and I think I know why,' he raged. 'Because you're a coward, Natasha. You're afraid to know the truth. If you had to face the terrible thing you did, you couldn't bear it. Everything could have been so different for us if you hadn't condemned me so quickly.'

She didn't reply. Something inside her choked the words back before they could escape.

'If you knew how I planned that day,' Mario said. 'I'd told you that I had something important to say to you. I was going to ask you not to go home, to stay with me, become my love.

'My relationship with Tania was never serious. She was a very experienced woman who surrounded herself with various male "friends". I knew I wasn't the only man in her life but it didn't trouble me because I wasn't in love with her and she wasn't in love with me.

'But when I met you, things changed. Suddenly I no longer wanted "a bit of fun". I wanted something serious and I wanted it with you. Nobody else. Just you. So I met up with Tania and I told her that we couldn't see each other any more.

'She was angry, but I thought she understood. Then it happened. She descended on us; you disappeared. If you could have seen what I went through trying to find you, how deep in despair I was—well, I guess you'd have enjoyed it.'

'I wouldn't have believed it,' she retorted. 'You? In despair, when you played the field so easily?'

'I'd done with playing the field. That life was all over for me. And if I could have explained that—made you understand... But what's the use? You only believe what you want to believe.'

She stared at him, trying to take in his incredible words. It was as though she'd become two people—one recoiling from him, one reaching out, longing to know more.

'Are you two there?' Giorgio's voice came along the corridor.

'We're here,' Mario called back.

'Ah, good.' Giorgio appeared around the corner. 'Time to get changed back into normal clothes. No more photographs today, but we're going to see Romeo's house.'

Natasha escaped to the dressing room and rid herself of the costume. It was a relief to don modern clothes and become herself again. Juliet could be banished, at least for a while.

The longer the better, she thought, staring into the mirror and brushing her hair fiercely so that it fell down over her shoulders. It looked like spun gold in the afternoon sunlight. Once Mario had made a joke about it; 'my dangerous blonde bombshell' he'd said in a teasing voice.

'I'm not dangerous,' she'd protested.

'You can be when you act on instinct. Some of your instincts could scare a man.'

'Do I scare you?' she'd teased.

'You could if I scared easily.'

Today he'd told her frankly that her head-strong temper had done much to part them.

Suppose I'd stayed to listen to his 'explanations', she thought. *Should I have done that? Should I have trusted him? No! No!'*

She scraped her hair back as tight as it would go. When she was satisfied with her appearance she went down to join them.

Romeo's house was just a few minutes away from Juliet's and could only be seen from the outside.

'It looks like a fortress,' she said, 'with those battlements.'

'A lot of buildings were created like that in those days,' Giorgio said. 'Half of the city was almost permanently at war with the other half, hence the fight between the Capulets and Montagues.'

'Buongiorno!'

A cry from a few feet away made them turn to see a man hailing them. He seemed to be in his forties, tall and strongly built, and Natasha recognised him as a member of the *Comunità* that she had met on the first evening.

'You should have told me you were coming,' he said, giving her a hug.

'I wasn't sure until the last minute,' Mario said.

'Come and have coffee with me. My hotel is just around the corner.'

As they walked there Giorgio dropped his voice to say to Natasha, 'Mario would have avoided this meeting if he could. That's Riccardo, the rival who tried to challenge him for the presidency of the *Comunità*. He's very wealthy, owns more vineyards than any of the others, and likes giving orders just as much as Mario does.'

'You said Mario got him to back off.'

'Yes. Not sure how, but the rumours say some of Riccardo's business dealings wouldn't bear inspection.'

'You mean Mario threatened him?'

'I doubt if it was a blatant threat. That isn't Mario's way. He'll just make a remark that only one man will understand—and fear. Riccardo dropped his challenge very suddenly. Mario isn't a man you tangle with, not if you've got any sense.'

Riccardo's premises were lavish and decorative, even more so than the Dimitri Hotel. Wherever Natasha looked she could see that money had been spent without restraint. It might well appear that Riccardo was a man who could challenge Mario, but after only a few minutes seeing them together Natasha sensed that this could never happen.

Riccardo was afraid of Mario. That was the incredible truth. And Mario was content to have it be so. The young man who had once enjoyed getting his own way by charm now used power to bend people to his will.

He had blamed her for disappearing, leaving him to search frantically until finally he had accepted despair. She had resisted the accusation, but now it troubled her more than she could face. This man scared other people, but admitted that she scared him.

She fell into earnest conversation with Riccardo.

'I want to see the rest of Verona,' she said. 'It's not just about *Romeo and Juliet*. There's more to life than romance.'

'No doubt about that,' Mario agreed.

They clinked glasses.

'Right,' Natasha said. 'I've done my preliminary work. Now I'm going to shut myself away for a while to get everything written. I'll see you in a few days, gentlemen.'

'So we're no longer needed?' Giorgio asked comically. 'You're dismissing us just like that? Ah, it's a hard world.'

'That's how it is,' Mario said, reflecting Giorgio's theatrical manner. 'A woman dismisses a man when she no longer needs him. We just have to accept it.'

They all laughed.

'If I'm not required for a while I'll go back to Venice for a few days,' Mario said. 'Sally, my sister-in-law, is about to give birth again. She had a hard time with her last baby so I think Damiano might appreciate having me around for a few days. I'll stay in touch—*signorina*, Giorgio will take care of you.'

'Thank you. If I have Giorgio, what more could I possibly want?'

Mario left that afternoon, bidding her a polite goodbye in front of everyone else, adding, 'Giorgio can contact me if need be. Goodbye, everyone.'

He fled.

CHAPTER SIX

IT WAS A relief for Natasha to spend the next few days without Mario. She needed time to come to terms with what he'd told her.

If you knew how I planned that day... I was going to ask you not to go home, to stay with me, become my love.

She tried to block out the memory, but it haunted her. Mario vowed he'd broken with Tania because he loved her and was preparing to tell her.

We didn't have to end up here. We could have been married by now, and expecting our first child. Instead—well, look at us.

She tried not to hear the terrible words echoing in her mind. Mario had accused her of believing only what she wanted to believe. And perhaps he was right. If he was telling the truth it meant that she had created the disaster almost single-handed.

To escape that unbearable thought, she submerged herself in work, studying not just Verona itself but its surroundings. It stood in the Veneto, the northern region of Italy that was best known for the city of Venice.

'That's why we speak Venetian here,' Giorgio told her.

'Venetian? Venice has its own language?'

'Certainly, and it's spoken throughout the Veneto. People speak Italian as well, and English is very common because of all the tourists. But you need to know about the Venetian language to really understand this area.'

'And that's what I want to do,' she said, scribbling furiously.

The next day the photographer delivered the pictures of 'Romeo and Juliet' and she studied them closely.

Mario's face fascinated her. When they had met a few days ago, she'd thought he looked older, harsher, more tense. But in these pictures he had changed again, becoming more like the young man she remembered. She thought she could see a softening in his expression as he looked at Juliet, a glow in his eyes which the camera had caught wonderfully.

She had seen that glow before, two years ago. *He must be a very good actor*, she thought. *But I suppose I knew that.*

She spent some time wandering Verona alone, drinking in the atmosphere with nobody to distract her. She found a street she thought might be the place where Juliet's cousin Tybalt killed Romeo's friend, Mercutio. Just a little further on was where Romeo could have caught up with Tybalt and stabbed him in revenge.

Nearby were two *Comunità* hotels, where she was welcomed eagerly. She looked them over, and jotted down notes in readiness for the next despatch.

There were a dozen places to visit, but she had no energy to explore further today. She had coped with the emotional strains of the last few days, but they had taken their toll. Now she was tired and her head ached a little, so she set off back to the Dimitri Hotel.

It was a relief to get back there, order a coffee and sit in the hotel café. She closed her eyes, unaware that a man was watching her a few yards away, taking in every detail about her: her air of despondency, her appearance of being apart from the world, her loneliness.

Suddenly she looked up and saw him.

'Mario!'

'Hello, Natasha.' He went to sit beside her.

'You're back from Venice then?'

'Yes, I arrived ten minutes ago.'

'Is everything all right with your family?'

'Yes, Sally came through it well and now I've got a niece.'

'Congratulations.'

'Thank you. How are things with you? You look very tired.'

'I've had a busy day, but a very satisfying one.'

'Did anyone go with you, to make sure you didn't get lost?'

'Hey, there's no need to insult me.'

'What?'

'I'm not some silly girl who gets lost every time she's in an unfamiliar street.'

'Sorry, ma'am.'

'I could have asked Giorgio to escort me, but I refused. I can manage.'

He had no doubt of her real meaning. She'd needed time alone, free of the tension that was always there between them. He understood because he felt the same.

'You work too hard,' he said. 'You always did. I remember once before, when we first met in Venice, you said you'd been working so hard that you were exhausted. I took you for a ride in a gondola, and you fell asleep.'

He said it with a smile but she recalled that he hadn't been amused at the time. He was used to taking girls for gondola rides, but not used to them nodding off in his company.

'You took me back to the hotel and said goodnight very firmly,' she recalled, smiling. 'You felt insulted at my behaviour. I always wondered what you did for the rest of the evening, but I expect you found someone else who managed to stay awake.'

'I can't remember,' he said firmly.

'Very tactful.'

They both laughed. He couldn't tell her that he'd spent the rest of that evening alone, brooding about her seeming indifference to his attentions. She had intrigued him, and he'd sought her out early next day.

'That was always the way with you,' he reflected now. 'There, yet not there, keeping me wondering.'

'I didn't do it on purpose,' she said. 'You thought I was being a deliberate tease, but I wasn't. I was wondering too.'

And that had been her attraction for him, he realised. Where other girls were often willing, sometimes too willing, Natasha had always been just out of reach. It had driven him crazy but it had kept him in pursuit of her. Until finally she had vanished, leaving him devastated.

How much had she really felt for him? To

this day he didn't know, and he doubted he ever would.

But one thing was certain. She was no longer the tense, nervy creature of a few days ago. The woman who had forced a kiss on him as revenge for his kissing her had simply vanished. Now she was relaxed, in command, humorous, alluring.

'I hear that you've been working hard,' he said. 'You've been contacting the other hotel owners to get information, and showing them what you planned to write so that they could approve it. They're very impressed. My stock has risen considerably since I performed the brilliant act of securing your services.' He gave a theatrical flourish. 'Only a genius like myself could have discovered you.'

'But you didn't discover me. It was Giorgio.'

'Hush. We don't say that.' He grinned. 'And neither does Giorgio if he knows what's good for him.'

'I see. The boss gives his orders and we all jump to obey.'

'Some do. I doubt I'll ever see the day when you jump to obey.'

'But you pay my wages,' she reminded him. 'Surely I have no choice but to obey you?'

'All right, all right. You've had your joke.'

'It's not a joke. You're my employer. I know

it's Giorgio who directs me, but you're the authority. If you told him to fire me, he'd have to do so.'

'There's no danger of that.'

'Actually, there's something I've been meaning to say to you.'

'What is it?' he asked with a sense of foreboding, for her tone implied a serious matter. 'Go on, tell me. How bad is it?'

'It's not bad at all. I want to say thank you.'

'Thank you? For what?' he asked, sounding nervous.

'For changing my contract so that I'm making more money. I couldn't believe it when Giorgio showed me the new one and said you'd told him to increase it.'

'But you've already thanked me,' he said. 'You did so a few minutes afterwards. I told you then that it was essential to secure your professional services.'

'Yes, you told me that, but you knew how bad my financial problems were. You could have secured me without raising the money. I think there may have been a little kindness involved too.'

He gave a slight smile. 'Kindness? Me? I'm a businessman. I don't do kindness.'

'I think you do. I can remember things in

Venice—that little girl who lost her dog, and you found it for her.'

'I was only trying to impress you.'

'And you succeeded. You don't like people to know about your kind and caring streak but it's there.'

'That's practically an insult.'

'Then you'll have to put up with me insulting you,' she said.

'I think I can just about manage that.'

'The thing is—that quarrel we had the other day, when we'd finished having the pictures taken… It just flared up but I wish it hadn't.'

'So do I. I said things I didn't mean.'

'You said I was afraid to face the truth, that everything could have been different if I'd listened to you. I think you meant that and I don't blame you.'

'But do you believe what I told you—about Tania, how I'd already broken with her?'

'Please—please don't,' she gasped. 'It's in the past. It doesn't matter now.'

'Meaning that you still don't believe me.'

'I don't know,' she said in anguish. 'There are so many things battling each other in my mind—'

'I know the feeling,' he said wryly.

'But it doesn't matter.'

'Natasha, how can it not matter? You always prided yourself on being logical, but if you think what happened between us didn't matter you're talking nonsense.'

'I didn't mean that. It mattered then, but not now. The world has moved on. We've moved on.'

'Ah, yes,' he said quietly. 'We've moved on.'

'And I think we were never meant to be together. Something was always fated to go wrong.'

'Now you sound like Giorgio.'

'What do you mean?'

'Just before you arrived, he and I were talking about Romeo and Juliet being "star-crossed lovers". Sometimes a couple is meant for each other but just can't get it together. They just have to accept that fate is against them.'

'Yes,' she said thoughtfully. 'You could say that fate was against us. My problem was that you had more women in your life than you could count. Or that I could count.'

'And mine was that you don't trust any man. I've always wondered why. Was there some other guy who walked out and broke your heart?'

'In a way, yes, but it's not how you think. The man who walked out was my father.'

She fell silent until he said, 'Tell me about him.'

'I loved him, and he loved me, so I thought.

And then he just vanished. I never heard from him again. We seemed to be so close but he just wiped me and my mother out of existence.'

As you did with me, Mario thought, but was too tactful to say.

'My mother was so bitter. She told me a million times that no man could ever be trusted, but she didn't need to say it. I felt it for myself.'

'So when we knew each other you were always reminding yourself that no man could be trusted—especially me.'

'No, not especially you. You mattered more than anyone else but—'

'But you instinctively thought I was no different from the rest of them. Except perhaps a bit worse.'

'No, no—it wasn't like that.'

'From where I'm sitting it was exactly like that.'

'And so you've come close to hating me,' she sighed. 'Perhaps I can't blame you.'

'Please, Natasha, forget I said that. I was in a temper. I wanted to hurt you because I resented the way you'd just shown your power over me. The way you kissed me made a point I didn't want to admit.'

'A point?' Her heart was beating fast.

'You showed me that I'm not the strong,

FREE Merchandise is 'in the Cards' for you!

Dear Reader,

We're giving away FREE MERCHANDISE!

Seriously, we'd like to reward you for reading this novel by giving you **FREE MERCHANDISE** worth over **$20**. And no purchase is necessary!

You see the Jack of Hearts sticker above? Paste that sticker in the box on the Free Merchandise Voucher inside. Return the Voucher promptly...and we'll send you valuable Free Merchandise!

Thanks again for reading one of our novels—and enjoy your Free Merchandise with our compliments!

Pam Powers

Pam Powers

P.S. Look inside to see what Free Merchandise is **"in the cards"** for you!

W e'd like to send you two free books like the one you are enjoying now. Your two books have a combined price of over $10, but they are yours to keep absolutely FREE! We'll even send you 2 wonderful surprise gifts. You can't lose!

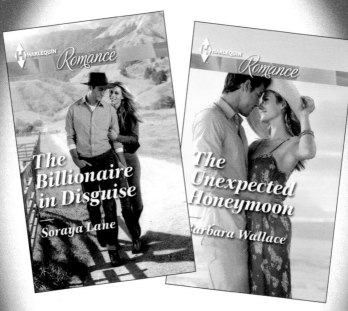

REMEMBER: Your Free Merchandise, consisting of **2 Free Books** and **2 Free Gifts**, is worth over $20.00! No purchase is necessary, so please send for your Free Merchandise today.

YOUR FREE MERCHANDISE INCLUDES...

2 FREE Books **AND** 2 FREE Mystery Gifts

▼ Detach card and mail today. No stamp needed. ▼

© 2013 HARLEQUIN ENTERPRISES LIMITED ® and ™ are trademarks owned and used by the trademark owner and/or its licensee. Printed in the U.S.A.

FREE MERCHANDISE VOUCHER

2 FREE BOOKS and 2 FREE GIFTS

Please send my Free Merchandise, consisting of
2 Free Books and **2 Free Mystery Gifts**.
I understand that I am under no obligation to buy
anything, as explained on the back of this card.

119/319 HDL GGA3

Please Print

FIRST NAME

LAST NAME

ADDRESS

APT.#   CITY

STATE/PROV.   ZIP/POSTAL CODE

Offer limited to one per household and not applicable to series that subscriber is currently receiving.
Your Privacy—The Harlequin® Reader Service is committed to protecting your privacy. Our Privacy Policy is available online at www.ReaderService.com or upon request from the Harlequin Reader Service. We make a portion of our mailing list available to reputable third parties that offer products we believe may interest you. If you prefer that we not exchange your name with third parties, or if you wish to clarify or modify your communication preferences, please visit us at www.ReaderService.com/consumerschoice or write to us at Harlequin Reader Service Preference Service, P.O. Box 9062, Buffalo, NY 14269. Include your complete name and address.

NO PURCHASE NECESSARY!

HR_215_FM13

independent fellow I like to believe I am. So I hit back with the worst thing I could think of. I didn't mean it and I'm not proud of it. Do you think you can forgive me?'

'That depends.'

'On what?' he asked cautiously.

'On whether *you* can forgive *me*.'

'There's nothing to forgive.'

'Really? What about the way you say I—?'

'Stop there,' he said quickly. 'Whatever I may have said, I take it back. It's over. It's done with. Let us be friends.'

She considered a moment before smiling and saying wistfully, 'That would be nice.'

'It's settled then.'

'Shake?' She held out her hand, but he fended her off.

'No. We shook hands the first night as professional associates. But now we're friends—and friends don't shake hands. They don't need to.' He leaned over and kissed her cheek. 'That's what friends do. And they buy each other coffee.'

'Good. Waiter!'

'No, I meant that I'd buy you a coffee.'

'Stop giving me orders. I'm buying and that's that.'

'Yes, ma'am. Anything you say, ma'am.'

'Mind you, you'll have to do the talking.'

He nodded, gave the waiter the order in Italian, then watched as she paid.

'Have you explored anywhere recently?' he asked.

'I've looked around a bit, but there's still one big place I've set my heart on visiting and that's Juliet's tomb.

'Now it's a museum,' she said. 'It seems to attract as many tourists as the balcony, so I must go there and plan the next article.'

'There's a *Comunità* hotel nearby,' Mario said. 'The Albergo Martinez. You met the owner the other night. We could dine there tonight and hear anything they have to say. Let me call him.'

He took out his phone, made a call and started talking in Italian. While she was waiting, her own mobile phone beeped. Her heart beat hard with horror when she read the text message.

After a few minutes Mario hung up, saying, 'He's expecting us in a couple of hours.'

He stopped suddenly, frowning as he saw her staring into space, full of tension.

'What is it?' he asked. 'What happened?'

'Nothing.'

'No, something's the matter. What is it?'

'No—no—I'm all right. I'd like to go to my room.'

She got up and walked quickly away. Frowning, he followed her, hurrying until he caught up and could take a firm hold of her hand. She didn't resist but neither did she respond, and he had a feeling that she had taken refuge in another world, from which he was excluded.

He accompanied her as far as her door, noting that she still looked pale and tense.

'I'll collect you in an hour,' he said.

'I'll be ready.'

Once inside, she undressed and got into the shower. There was a kind of relief in being doused with water, as though it could wash away the shock that had overtaken her.

The text on her mobile phone had been from Elroy Jenson:

You won't get away from me.

He's driving me crazy, she told herself. *And that's what he wants*.

She wondered why she hadn't told Mario what had troubled her. It should have been easy since she had already told him about Elroy, and he would have been a valuable ally. But something in her was reluctant to reveal more vulnerability. Especially to Mario.

When she had showered she put on a neat

dark blue dress, suitable for a polite gathering. For several minutes she teased her hair, trying to decide whether to be seductive or businesslike. As so often with Mario, her mind was filled with conflicting thoughts.

Their conversation had been fraught with double meanings. He'd said, *I wanted to hurt you because I resented the way you'd just shown your power over me.*

But he'd implied the power of a bully, not of a woman. They had made a truce, but the battle was far from over.

When he'd pressed her to say that she believed him now she had been unable to say what he wanted to hear. She longed to believe him, but she couldn't quite make herself take the final step.

But why should it matter whether I believe him or not? she mused. *That's all over. What matters is that we can manage to be friends.*

Nico was watching for their arrival at the Albergo Martinez and came to meet them with hands outstretched. Natasha recognised him from their meeting the first night.

Over supper he described the tomb.

'Juliet was buried in the church of San Francesco al Corso, a monastery,' he explained.

'Yes, it was Friar Laurence, a monk, who

married them,' Natasha recalled. 'On their wedding day they went to his cell and he took them to the church to marry them.'

'True. And when Juliet died—or at least she'd drunk the potion and seemed dead— she was taken to the monastery to be buried. These days the monastery has become a museum. You can go to the crypt and see the sarcophagus that legend says was hers.

'The museum also hosts weddings. Many people choose to become united for life in the place where Romeo and Juliet were united in eternity. Of course, if they are seeking a hotel not too far away—'

'They'll be glad to discover yours,' she said in her most professional manner. 'I shall make sure that they do.'

'*Eccellente!* Mario, you've made a fine discovery in this talented lady. Don't let her go, whatever you do.'

'Don't worry; I won't,' he said with a cheerful nod.

'Now, let us go in to supper.'

Supper was served at a large table where many people were already sitting. As they sat down Natasha became aware of something she had seen many times before. From every direction women were casting admiring glances at Mario. It had been there from the beginning, two years ago. It was still there.

And why not? she thought. *He's got the looks to make it happen. And it doesn't bother me any more.*

She soon discovered that the man sitting next to her was an ideal choice. His name was Tonio and he was an academic, specialising in English history. As history had always been one of her interests, she was soon deep in conversation with him, intrigued by his prejudiced arguments.

'You're all wrong about Richard III,' she told him. 'Shakespeare depicted him as a monster but he wasn't really—'

'You English!' he exclaimed. 'You can never believe that any of your monarchs were evil.'

'On the contrary, the evil ones are the most fun. But Richard's evil reputation is mostly a kind of show business.'

'I've studied the evidence and I tell you—'

Heads close together, they stayed absorbed in their argument, with the rest of the table regarding them with amused fascination. All except Mario, who was looking displeased, which surprised Natasha when she happened to glance up. The luscious beauty beside him was paying him fervent attention that a man might be expected to enjoy. But he seemed to be tolerating rather than encouraging her.

'I see Bianca's got her claws into a new man,' said Tonio, sounding amused.

'You speak as though it happens often.'

'With Bianca it does. She likes to cast her net wide.'

'It doesn't look as though he's fallen under her spell.'

'Not now, but give him a little time.'

Bianca was clearly a practised flirt, convinced that any man was hers for the asking. When she patted Mario's face, giggling, he smiled back politely before returning his gaze to Natasha.

'You need to look at it like this,' Tonio said, returning to their discussion. 'King Richard couldn't possibly—'

She plunged back into the argument, enjoying herself for the next half hour, until somebody put on some music and people began to dance. Suddenly Mario appeared by her chair.

'Dance with me,' he said.

'Wouldn't you rather dance with Bianca?'

'No.' He grasped her hand, drew her to her feet and onto the floor.

'I thought you were having a lovely time.' She laughed as they twirled.

'Did you really?' he demanded ironically.

'Being hunted down by a woman who'd gladly have given you anything you wanted.'

'Which would be fine if there was anything I did want from her. But I don't.'

'That wouldn't stop some men. They'd just take anything that's going.'

'I was like that once, when I was young and stupid. I grew up in the end, but by then it was too late.'

He said the last words with a wry look. The next moment the temptress glided past them. She was dancing with another man, but even so she gave Mario a glance that made him tighten his grasp on Natasha.

'Rescue me,' he growled.

'How?'

'Anyhow.'

'All right. Here goes. Aaaargh!'

With a theatrical sigh, she drooped against his chest.

'Oh, how my head aches,' she declared. 'I really must go home.'

'I'll take you,' he said.

Turning to their host, he explained that it was necessary to take Natasha away at once.

'She isn't feeling well,' he said. 'She must go to bed.'

From somewhere came the sound of choking laughter. Mario ignored it and picked Natasha up to carry her from the room. He didn't set her down until they reached the car.

'Thank you,' he said as they drove away.

'No problem. I'm really glad to leave because I need some sleep. Of course, if you want to go back and spend time with Bianca—'

'If that's your idea of a joke, it's not funny,' he said in an edgy voice.

'Sorry, I couldn't resist it.'

'Perhaps you should try to resist it. I'm just a sitting duck as far as you're concerned.'

'All right, I apologise.'

'It was getting very difficult in there.'

'You know what they're all thinking now, don't you?' she chuckled.

'Yes, they think that when we get home we're going to— Well, you can imagine.'

'Yes, I can imagine.'

'And I'm sorry. But that woman was getting embarrassing.'

'Don't tell me you're afraid of her. You? A man who's afraid of nothing.'

'You'd be surprised at some of the things I'm afraid of,' he said. 'Once you were one of them. Now you're beginning to feel like the best friend I have.'

'Good. Then we have nothing left to worry about…'

CHAPTER SEVEN

NEXT MORNING THEY drove to the monastery museum and went down into the crypt, where several other tourists had already gathered, looking at a large marble sarcophagus.

It was open at the top, revealing that it was empty now, but legend said that this was where Juliet had lain after taking the drug that made her appear lifeless. Here, Romeo had come to find her and, believing her dead, had taken his own life, minutes before she awoke. Finding him dead, she had taken her own life.

'I just don't understand it,' said an elderly man, staring into the sarcophagus. 'How could two people so young take their own lives?'

'Maybe they didn't,' said one of his companions. 'Maybe that's an invention of the story.'

'No,' Natasha said. 'It's part of the story

because it was inevitable. It's what you do if life has lost all meaning.'

'And that can happen at any age,' Mario said at once.

'No,' the old man said. 'They could have got over each other and found other lovers.'

'But they didn't believe that,' Mario pointed out.

'Youngsters never do,' the man said loftily. 'But when they get older they find out that nothing ever really matters that much. Love comes and goes and comes again. It's ridiculous to believe anyone discovers the full meaning of their life as young as that.'

'No,' Mario said. 'It's ridiculous to believe that such a discovery happens to a timetable. It happens when it's ready to happen. Not before and not after.'

The old man looked at him with interest. 'You sound like an expert, sir.'

'I guess we're all experts, one way or another,' Mario said.

There were some murmurs of agreement from the little crowd as they turned away, following their tourist guide to another part of the museum.

Now that they were alone, Mario watched as Natasha looked into the sarcophagus.

'They married and had one sweet night together,' she murmured. 'But when they finally lay together it was here.'

'They lie together and they always will,' Mario said.

She turned a smiling face on him. 'You know what you've done, don't you?'

'What have I done?'

'Given me a wonderful idea that I can develop for the piece I'm writing. "They lie together and they always will." Thank you.'

He made an ironic gesture. 'Glad to be of use.'

'Would you mind leaving me alone here for a while? I just want to—' She looked around her, taking a deep breath, her arms extended.

She just wanted to absorb a romantic atmosphere without being troubled by his presence, he thought. A dreary inconvenience. That was how she saw him now.

True, she had kissed him, but in anger, not in love or desire. And hell would freeze over before he let her suspect the depth of her triumph.

He stepped aside to a place in the shadows. From here he saw her stare down again into the tomb, reaching out into the empty space inside. What did she see in that space? Romeo, lying there, waiting for her to join him? Or Romeo and Juliet, sleeping eternally, clasped in each other's arms, held against each other's hearts?

Whatever it was, she had not invited him to be with her, because in her heart she was certain that he had left the dream behind long ago. If he had ever believed in it.

If only there was some magic spell that could enable her to look into his heart and see the truth he had carried there ever since their first meeting. Might she then look at him with eyes as fervent and glowing as she had done once, long, long ago?

He stayed watching her for a while, expecting that any moment she would move away. But she seemed transfixed, and at last he went to her.

'Are you all right?' he asked. 'You seem almost troubled.'

'No, I'm not troubled. It's just the atmosphere here, and what this tomb represents.'

'Surely it just represents death?'

'No, there's more. Finality, fulfilment, completion. They were young; they could have gone on and had lives that would have seemed satisfying. But each meant more to the other than life itself. You put it perfectly when you said people can discover what really matters while they're still young, and then they lie together for ever. This—'

she looked around at the walls of the tomb '—this says everything.'

'I think we should go now,' he said. Her fascination with the place was making him uneasy.

'Yes, I've done all I need to do here. I'll spend this evening working on it. Then I'll do a new article and send it around the *Comunità*, so they can tell me what they think. I'm sure their suggestions will be useful.'

'I see you've got all the boxes ticked.'

'I hope so. That's what you're paying me for. Shall we go? We're finished here, aren't we?'

'Oh, yes,' he agreed. 'We're finished here.'

No more was said on the way back to the hotel.

Once there, Natasha hurried up to her room to get to work. She had supper served to her there and did not go downstairs all evening. She needed to be alone to think about the day. Mario's observations at the tomb had left her wondering. The old man had said he sounded like an expert about love. Mario had replied, *We're all experts, one way or another.*

One way or another. Love might be a joy or a betrayal. Which had he meant?

But I don't need to ask that, she thought.

He feels betrayed, just as I do. But how is that possible? Can we have both betrayed each other?

He'd accused her of refusing to listen to him because she feared the truth, feared to confront her own part in their break-up. She had denied it, but could there possibly be a grain of truth in it?

Surely not, she thought. It couldn't have turned out any differently. Could it?

She had felt her own pain so intensely, but now she was confronted by his pain and it was a bewildering experience.

We'll never understand each other, she thought. *I mustn't hope for too much. Or do I mean fear too much?*

She gave herself a mental shake.

That's enough. I'm here to work and when I've finished my job I'll leave, whatever he says or does.

But the next day everything changed.

In the morning she went exploring again, wandering Verona on foot until, in the afternoon, she reached Juliet's house. There, she looked around the courtyard, meaning to go inside and see the museum.

But something drew her to Juliet's statue,

still standing as it had been before, gazing into the distance.

If only, she thought, she could indulge the fantasy of asking Juliet's advice, and imagining an answer. It might help sort out the confusion in her head and her heart.

She didn't know how Mario felt, or how she herself felt. When he had kissed her she'd wanted him so much that it scared her. So she had punished him with a kiss designed to show him what he'd lost. But she too had been reminded of what she'd lost.

Into her mind came Mario's face, looking as he had at the start of the photo shoot. His expression had been—she struggled for the words—cautious, perhaps a little nervous.

She had blamed him for kissing her, thinking him too confident and self-satisfied. But did she blame him too much? Had he been uneasy, secretly wanting the kiss but unsure of himself?

I know how that feels, she brooded. *In my heart I wanted him to kiss me. Perhaps that's why I was so angry when he did.*

She sighed and turned away. Then she stopped, tense.

Mario was standing there, watching her.

'I happened to see you in the street,' he

said, 'so I took the liberty of following you. Have you been inside the house?'

'No, I was about to go in.'

'Let's go in together.'

Inside, they looked briefly around the sixteenth-century furniture, absorbing the perfect atmosphere for the legend. Then they climbed the stairs and stepped out onto the balcony.

A young couple was already there, wrapped in each other's arms.

'Sorry,' the girl said, moving aside. 'We just had to come and see it again. We're getting married here next week and all the pictures will be taken out on the balcony.'

'How lovely,' Natasha said. 'The perfect place.'

'We thought so.' They kissed and slipped away into the building.

How lucky they were, she thought, to be so sure of each other, of life, of the future.

Now the light was fading, and there were few visitors. It was easy to imagine herself as Juliet, standing there looking into the night sky, unaware that Romeo was down below, watching her.

'I wonder what it was like for her,' she mused, 'to stand here, dreaming of him, then finally realising he was there, seeing him watching her, not knowing that their love was fated.'

Before he could answer, there was a shrill from her mobile phone. But she ignored it.

'Aren't you going to answer that?' Mario asked.

'No, it can wait,' she said in a tense voice. 'I didn't mean to bring it with me. I don't want to be distracted.'

The phone shrilled again.

'Answer it,' Mario said. 'Get rid of them.'

Reluctantly, she pulled out the phone and answered.

'At last,' said the voice she dreaded.

'You again,' she snapped. 'Stop pestering me.'

'Stop telling me what to do,' said Jenson's voice. 'If I want to call you I shall. Who do you think you are to give me orders?'

'Who do I think I am? I'm the woman who told you to go and jump in the lake. I'm the woman who wants nothing to do with a man as disgusting as you. You should have realised that by now.'

From the other end of the line came a crack of laughter.

'No, you're the one who should have woken up to reality, you stupid tart. You don't know what I could do to you—'

'I think I do. You've made it brutally clear.'

'That was just the start. You don't know how sorry I can make you, but you're going to find out. I know something about you, Natasha, and by the time I've finished you're going to wish you'd treated me with more respect.'

Before she could reply, the phone was wrenched from her hand by Mario.

'Jenson,' he snapped. 'Go to hell. Leave her alone or I'll make you sorry.'

A bellow of ugly laughter reached him down the line.

'Not as sorry as you'll be if you're involved with Natasha,' Jenson bawled. 'She's made herself my enemy, and if you side with her you'll be my enemy too. I have a way with enemies.'

With a swift movement Mario severed the connection.

'Jenson's still pestering you?'

'Yes, he won't stop.' She was shaking.

'All right, let's deal with this,' Mario said. He put his arms around her firmly, protectively. 'Come on, we're going back to the hotel.'

Still holding her, he led her back to his car. She almost collapsed into the seat beside him and sat with her head in her hands during the drive. To his relief, there was almost nobody in the hotel lobby and he was able to take her upstairs quickly. As soon as the door closed behind them he clasped her once more in his arms.

'It's all right,' he said fiercely. 'There's nothing to be scared of. You're safe here. Jenson is in the past.'

'No, he's not,' she groaned. 'As long as he can reach me he's not in the past. Changing my number is useless. He always finds out my new one. That's how powerful he is. I'm scared. He haunts me. When I get a text or a call from him it's as though he's actually there. He's already ruined my career, and I can't be rid of him.'

'You're wrong,' Mario said. 'He hasn't ruined your career, and he isn't going to because I'm not going to let him.'

She took some deep breaths, managing to calm down a little. Mario touched her chin, lifting it so that he could see her face. For a moment he was tempted to give her a gentle kiss, by way of comfort. But, instead, he took her to the bed, still holding her as she sat down, then drawing her head against him again.

'Thank goodness you were there,' she said. 'I couldn't have coped alone.'

'I know you couldn't,' he said morosely. 'That's why I grabbed your phone in a way you must have thought rather rude. If something threatens me I like to know how serious it is.'

'But he's not threatening you.'

'Anything that threatens you threatens me. I told you—I'll deal with it.'

'Thank you.' She clung to him. 'It's lucky it was only a phone call. If he'd turned up in person I think I'd have done something violent, perhaps strangled him.' She made a wry face. 'You're right in what you've always said about my nasty temper.'

'I've never said it was a nasty temper,' he disclaimed at once. 'It's a quick temper. Act first, think later.'

'By which time it's too late to think,' she sighed.

He didn't reply, merely tightened his arms about her.

'It's been a curse all my life,' she said. 'My mother used to say I'd come to a bad end. According to her, I got my temper from my father, and I never heard her say a good word about him.'

'You mentioned him the other day. Didn't they split up?'

'He left her when I was only ten. Just

walked out and vanished. It broke my heart. Until then I'd had a wonderful relationship with my father. I was the apple of his eye. But he left my mother for another woman and I never heard from him again.'

'Never? Are you sure your mother didn't keep you apart?'

'No, he didn't write or call. I used to watch the mail arrive and there was never anything from him. I tried telephoning him but he'd changed his number.'

He didn't reply. She waited for him to remind her how she'd done the same thing, but he only hugged her closer.

'You should put all that behind you,' he murmured. 'The past is gone, but you must make sure it *is* the past. Don't let it haunt your life, or it will control you.'

'You sound as though you really know,' she said.

'In a way I do. At one time I owed so much to Damiano that the need to get free and grow up became the most important thing in my life.'

'Grow up?'

'I took a long time to get to that stage.'

That was true, she thought, remembering him two years ago. Now he was so much stronger and more serious that he was almost a different man.

'"Haunt your life",' she murmured. 'My mother never got over him abandoning us. She told me again and again that you could never trust a man.'

'And her words have stayed with you always,' he said softly.

'Not just her words. It was also the way he cut me out of his life, after I'd seemed to mean so much to him. I'd believed in his love, but it meant nothing.'

Mario uttered a soft curse. 'I wish I had him here so that I could sock him in the jaw,' he said. 'But don't let your father—or Elroy Jenson—destroy your life, Natasha. Banish them into the past, turn your back and become the person you really are.'

'Too late,' she sighed.

'It's never too late if it's what you really want.'

She would have given anything to see his face as he uttered those words, but her head was pressed against his shoulder.

'Never too late,' she echoed, resting against him. A feeling of sleepy contentment was overtaking her, and she could have happily stayed like this for ever.

Mario sensed the moment when she began

to doze. He tightened his arms about her, laying his lips against her hair, feeling an unfamiliar warmth go through him. He wanted to hold her close, but not in the hope of making love with her, only to keep her safe.

It was a feeling he'd never known before. When they had first met she had seemed strong, full of confidence, able to challenge the world and emerge victorious.

He found his mind drifting back to his own past. Since the day he'd first begun flirting with girlfriends he had never been attracted by commitment. His girlfriends had all been strong, independent, fancying him but not needing him.

Immature, he thought now wryly. *Boy, was I immature.*

Four years earlier he'd met Sally, the woman who had married his brother, Damiano. His feelings for her had grown so deep that he'd fled their home in Venice for safety's sake.

Later, he'd felt safe enough to return occasionally. His interest in the hotel business had grown. Damiano had been an excellent teacher and Mario's talent had flourished until he could manage to buy and run his own hotel. But he'd remained a playboy, dancing from girl to girl, never choosing anyone who might seriously need him.

Now he realised how much things had changed. Natasha's sadness had touched his heart. She was alone and vulnerable, and the knowledge affected him strongly. The torment he'd endured when she'd deserted him had begun to fade, overwhelmed by her need. She needed a friend to be strong for her, and something told him that he should be that person because without him she had nobody. He tightened his arms, trying to send her a silent message of reassurance. Her breathing was steady and, although he couldn't see her face, he guessed she was still dozing.

Probably just as well that they couldn't talk, he thought. Words could be a trap, especially for a man like himself, with little verbal skill. He preferred to be judged by his actions rather than his words.

Since the day she'd arrived he knew he'd been clumsy, confused. The feeling had been increased by the suspicion that she enjoyed confusing him. He'd fought back, making matters worse, he now realised. But now he knew that his own feelings didn't matter. He only wanted her to feel safe.

He eased her down onto the bed. Her head drooped to one side and her eyes were closed, as though she'd slipped away from him into another world. And yet she was still with him.

And she always would be, he resolved. He'd lost her once. He couldn't bear to lose her again. He knew he had to keep her, but for the moment he must be silent about his decision. They had far to travel before things could be said openly between them.

Moving carefully, he lay down beside her, still holding her so that her head rested against him. For a while she was still, but then her arm moved, drifting slowly across his chest as though seeking him, his help and comfort.

For a moment he thought that she might awaken and he could say some of the things in his heart. But then she grew still again, and he knew she'd slipped back into another world. One where he did not exist, he realised. Did he exist for her at all?

He looked closely into her face, hoping to read in it some hint of an answer, but she was fast asleep. Their time would come, but for now he knew he must be patient. He closed his eyes.

In the early morning light Natasha opened her eyes to find herself in a strange world, one where her head rested against Mario and his arms enfolded her protectively.

At once she knew it was a dream. It could be nothing else.

'All right?' asked his gentle voice. 'Are you awake at last?'

'Am I—what—what am I—?'

Mario saw the dismay come into her eyes as she realised that she was lying in his arms.

'You've had a good night's sleep,' he said. 'So have I.'

'What happened? How did we—?'

'How did we end up lying together? You got a call from Jenson and it scared you. You were so upset that it seemed best not to leave you alone, so I came in here and stayed with you. But don't worry. I was just being a friend. I haven't done anything I shouldn't.'

She knew at once that it was true. Her flesh was calm and rested in a way that wouldn't have been true if he'd touched her sexually. He had merely held her gently, comfortingly in his arms, thinking only of her welfare.

'Truly,' he said. 'Stop worrying.'

'I'm not worried. I'm just glad you're here.'

'Glad?' he echoed. 'Really glad?'

'Of course. How could I not be? You said you'd keep me safe and you did. Oh, if I could only tell you how good that feels.'

'If that's what you want, that's all that matters,' he said.

Her eyes glowed and he became tense. Desire was growing in him. He wanted to kiss her smiling mouth, caress her warm body, feel her come to new life in his arms. But he had just reassured her that he had no such temptations, and her reaction left no doubt that this was what she wanted to hear.

He wanted her, but she didn't want him in the same way. That was what he had to accept. It was all he could do for her.

She stirred in his arms and he loosened his hold, thinking she was trying to move away from him. But she turned more towards him, closing her eyes again, sliding an arm around his body and murmuring, *'Mmm!'* as though she had discovered blissful contentment.

And that was what he brought her, he reflected. It was a kind of happiness, and better than the anguish of their first encounter, days ago.

'But there could be more,' he whispered softly into her ear.

'Mmm?'

'If we're patient, there could be more between us, surely? We could take it slowly, and then—maybe—'

'Maybe what?' she murmured.

'I know we still have things to put behind us, and it won't be easy. You didn't treat me kindly, vanishing like that, but, after the way your father behaved, I guess you don't trust any of us. And I hurt you but I didn't mean to. If only you could bring yourself to believe me about that. But you will. One day I just know you will, and then everything will be wonderful.'

'Mmm.'

He gave a gentle laugh. 'I wonder what "Mmm" actually means.'

She met his eyes. 'If I knew—I'd tell you.'

'No, you wouldn't. You enjoy keeping me guessing. All right. I'll play your game because the prize we could win is worth everything.'

'Yes,' she whispered. 'But will we win it?'

'Who knows?' he said. 'We *will* know. We must. But not just yet. Something will happen. It will make everything clear—soon—soon.'

'I guess you understand more than I do. You'll tell me when the time comes—whenever that is.'

She smiled at him in a way that filled him with hope.

CHAPTER EIGHT

'I'LL LEAVE YOU now so you can get some more sleep,' Mario said. 'See you in the morning.'

He fled from the room, downstairs and out into the garden. It was just becoming light and he went to the river, where he could lean over the wall and stare into the water, brooding.

It felt wonderful to have achieved a brief emotional contact with her, but he wondered how completely she understood him. He'd spoken of his hopes for the future, but were they any more than fantasies? She had said that something would happen. But when? How long must they wait to be sure?

He looked back at the building, where he could identify her room from the faint light that still glowed inside. As he watched, the floor-length window opened and she came out onto the balcony.

He backed away into the shadows so that

she wouldn't see him, but she didn't even look down. She stood motionless, her eyes turned up to the heavens as though she could find the answer to a mystery in that distant place.

Watching her on the balcony, he thought that this must have been how it was for Romeo, seeing his beloved standing there above him.

On the night she'd arrived he'd gone to stand beneath her window, looking up, longing to see her. And there she had been, reaching out into the night, her body full of anguish, speaking words he had strained to hear. Then she'd gone inside again, leaving him standing alone in the darkness, struggling to come to terms with his conflicting feelings.

Now, here he was again, watching Natasha from a distance, condemned perhaps to be always at a distance, unable to voice his emotions openly.

Romeo's words came into his head. *It is my lady, Oh, it is my love! Oh, that she knew she were!*

'Yes,' he murmured. 'It is my love. Oh, that she knew she were.'

She does know, argued a voice in his head. *You've made it very clear.*

But does she want to know? queried another voice. *Is she ready to accept?*

Her voice was still there in his mind, asking if they would win the prize. That alarmed him, as it meant she could envisage a future apart. The way ahead was still strewn with doubts and problems, and who knew what the answers would be? Or if there would be any answers?

Romeo had reached out from beneath Juliet's balcony, letting her know he was there, telling her of his feelings. But Mario knew that path wasn't open to him at this moment.

Slowly he backed away, retreating deep into the shadows, never taking his eyes off her.

For a while, she stayed looking up into the sky, but then she lowered her head and wrapped her arms about herself, leaning against the wall. Her demeanour suggested confusion, sadness. Mario drew in his breath sharply. He'd tried to ease those feelings in her, and had briefly thought he'd succeeded. But she was still lonely, still vulnerable, and the sight hurt him.

Once he could have reached out to console her openly, revealing everything in his heart, inviting her in, rejoicing in the unity they had seemed to share.

But that unity had been an illusion, with traps along the way, ready to bring them both down. She needed him. He felt this as he had never felt it before, and the longing to fulfil her need was taking him over, heart and soul. But her feelings for him, whatever they might be, were undermined by a caution that barred her from believing that she was his love.

'Oh, that she knew she were,' he whispered again. 'Oh, that I could convince her.'

He slipped quietly away for fear that she might see him.

Inside the hotel, he found Giorgio waiting for him in a state of agitation.

'You were right about her all along,' he said.

'Right about who?'

'Her. Natasha Bates. You suspected something troubling about her as soon as she arrived. You said you hadn't met her before but it was obvious you guessed what a suspicious character she was. And she knew that you sensed it. That's why she's so edgy when you're around.'

'What the devil are you talking about?' Mario snapped.

'We've received an email about Natasha that you must see. It's from Jenson Publications.'

'Show me.'

The email was blunt and vicious:

You should be warned about your employee, Natasha Bates. She's well known in the media business for her dishonesty and inefficiency. If you are wise you will dismiss her at once.

There was no name attached. The missive merely came from the Jenson Publications head office.

'He didn't dare put his name to it,' Mario growled. 'But this comes from Elroy Jenson, a miserable, scheming bastard who I'll strangle if I ever get my hands on him.'

'But suppose it's true,' Giorgio argued. 'You've always sensed that she was dodgy.'

'Don't you dare say that,' Mario raged. 'None of this is true and if I ever hear you say such a thing again I'll make you sorry.'

'All right, all right,' Giorgio said, hastily backing off, alarmed by the look in Mario's eyes. 'My lips are sealed.'

'Don't say it and don't even think it,' Mario snapped. 'Understand?'

'Understand,' Giorgio said. 'Sorry. It just hadn't occurred to me.'

'Yes, there are a lot of things that hadn't occurred to me either,' Mario sighed. 'But when they do occur—well, you just have to face them. This email is a pack of lies. Jenson came on to her, she rejected him and now he's out to destroy her out of spite.'

Giorgio nodded as comprehension came to him. 'So you're on her side?'

'Yes,' Mario said slowly. 'I'm on her side.'

In the past few days he'd felt a desire to care for Natasha, but those moments were nothing compared to the storm of protectiveness that invaded him now. If Jenson had been there in person he would have throttled him without compunction.

'Don't tell her about this,' he instructed Giorgio. 'He's trying to scare her and I won't have it.'

'But shouldn't we warn her? She should know she's got an enemy.'

'She already knows. But she also has us, and we're going to take care of her. Not a word. I don't want her upset.'

She had every reason to be upset, he realised. Elroy Jenson might not be following her physically, but he was after her in a far more dangerous way. Through stretching out his tentacles of power across the world, he thought he could still make her suffer for defying him.

But he was wrong, Mario thought angrily.

Now Natasha had him to defend her and he would do so, whatever it cost him.

'She mustn't suspect anything,' he said to Giorgio.

'If you say so.' Giorgio sighed reluctantly. 'But can we fend this man off?'

'We can and we will. She's going to be safe.' His face became set. 'I've promised her that and I'm going to keep my word.'

Turning back into her room from the balcony, Natasha returned to the bed and lay down. She had a strange yet pleasant feeling that Mario was still with her, whispering reassurances in her mind, or merely tightening his arms protectively around her, so that she understood.

But was that what he'd meant, or was she just listening to her own hopes? She was still wondering as she fell asleep.

She awoke feeling refreshed, eager to get up and face the day.

As soon as she swung her legs out of bed she knew something was wrong. The carpet beneath her feet was wet. Looking further, she found that the water came from the bathroom and covered most of the floor.

'Oh, heavens, I must have left a tap on!' she exclaimed in dismay.

But when exploring the bathroom she discovered not a tap but a leaking pipe, spilling water directly onto the floor.

Hastily, she called Mario and explained that she'd need a plumber. He arrived a few minutes later and swore when he saw the extent of the damage.

'This must be fixed quickly before it sinks through the floor,' he said. 'Pack your things and get out of here fast. I'll arrange another room for you.'

She was packed and finished in half an hour, glad to escape and leave the room to the plumbers who'd arrived. She found Mario waiting for her downstairs with a table laid for breakfast.

'There's a bit of a problem,' he said. 'It's high season and every room in the place is taken.'

'So I'll find a room somewhere else.'

'Certainly not. I have an apartment upstairs that you can have. I don't sleep there so the bed is free. You can relax in peace.'

'And do some work,' she said, gathering up her laptop.

His apartment was mainly a place of storage, filled with shelves and filing cabinets. She arrived to find a maid making up the bed.

'It's all yours,' Mario said. 'I'll leave you to it. Goodbye for now.'

She worked contentedly, sending her material to a dozen different sources. Then she felt the need for a short break, and crossed the room to switch on the television. But on the way her heel tangled in the carpet and she pitched forward. Reaching out, she grabbed hold of some small shelves, which promptly disgorged their contents onto the floor. With an exclamation, she dropped down and began gathering them up.

Then she stopped suddenly, as though something had grabbed her in a vice. An envelope had opened, spilling out several sheets of pale blue notepaper. On one of them she saw what was written at the bottom: *Your loving Tania.*

Her whole being was consumed by a silent howl of anguish. Tania was still communicating with Mario. After all his promises, his assurances that he had broken with her, that she meant nothing to him, the truth was that he had been in contact with her.

When she thought of how close she had come to trusting him she wanted to bang her head against the wall.

'Fool!' she murmured. 'Fool! You were so

wise in the beginning. You should have listened to your suspicions.'

Was he still in touch with her? Or was it an old letter? If so, why had he kept it so long?

Because he's still involved with her, she told herself. *He's been lying all this time.*

With frenzied hands she pulled the letter open and began to read it. As she read she grew still. When she got to the end she went back and read it again. And then again, trying to believe the incredible words Tania had written.

> *Don't keep me at a distance. I know you told me it was over because you wanted to be with that English girl, but look what she did when she found out about me. She wouldn't have vanished if she'd really loved you. I thought you'd realise that and come back to me. Why won't you take my calls or answer my emails?*
>
> *Don't keep rejecting me, Mario. Natasha can't possibly mean that much to you.*
>
> *Your loving Tania*

She read it again, murmuring the words aloud, as though in this way she could manage to convince herself that they were real.

Everything Mario had told her was true. He had broken with Tania, as he'd vowed. She had refused to accept it and kept hounding him, but it seemed that nothing would make him take her back.

'I should have believed you,' she whispered. 'Oh, my love, I should have trusted you. But why didn't you show me this? Then I would have known the truth.'

She noticed that the letter was written in English, and remembered how Tania had spoken mostly in English with the odd Italian word thrown in. Doubtless, English was her native language, and perhaps her closeness to Mario had helped his mastery of English.

Which is lucky, she thought. *If Tania had written in Italian I couldn't have understood, and I wouldn't have missed this for the world.*

A noise outside warned her that Mario was coming. Swiftly she gathered up the papers and thrust them back onto the shelf, except for the Tania letter, which she thrust into her pocket. She would want to read that again, many times.

Natasha was back in front of the computer when he came in.

'Did you manage to sort the plumbing problem?' she asked.

'Yes, it's all taken care of. It'll be a couple of days before you can move back in but, thanks to you, I was alerted in time to avoid total disaster. How are you getting on?'

'I've managed to do quite a lot of work. Now I feel like taking the evening off. I think I'll have a stroll by the river.'

'Am I allowed to come with you?'

'Why not?'

It was a joy to have his company now that she could see him in a new light. All the pain and tension of the past two years had vanished, leaving only happiness and hope.

The light was fading as they left the building and crossed the street to the river. He slipped his arm around her shoulders, and she stretched hers about his waist. Clinging together, they strolled along the bank until they reached a café by the water, and he indicated for her to sit down. Waving a waiter over, Mario spoke to him quickly in Italian and moments later the waiter returned with a bottle of wine.

'I have a reason for bringing you here,' Mario said. 'This place buys all its wine from a shop that stocks products from my vineyard.'

'The best, naturally,' she said.

'Naturally. Everyone knows about Verona's

romantic reputation, but its fame as a great wine centre tends to get blocked out.'

'I've been reading a little about it recently,' she said. 'There are wine tours, aren't there? We might do a little publicity for them too.'

'Good idea. You can turn your talents on to Vinitaly. That's a wine festival that happens every year in spring.' He grinned. 'There's a lot more to Verona than you think.'

'I'm sure there is. I look forward to discovering all its secrets.'

He raised his glass to her, saying, *'Ti vol un altro goto de vin?'*

'Is that Venetian?'

'You know about Venetian?'

'Giorgio told me. The more I know, the better.'

'It means would you like some more wine?'

'Yes, please. It's delicious.'

She sipped the wine, enjoying its excellent taste and the feeling that things might be going well at last.

He watched her, wondering at the smile on her face, unwilling to ask about it. There might be more pleasure in wondering.

When at last they rose and walked on he put an arm around her shoulder, saying, 'Are you all right? Not too cold?'

'I'm all right,' she said, looking up. 'Not

too cold, not too anything. Everything's perfect.'

He gave a soft chuckle. 'Does that mean I haven't offended you recently?'

She looked up at him teasingly. 'Not that I can think of.'

'You can usually think of something.'

They smiled and moved on.

She barely noticed where they were going. It was like being in a new world. Nothing was the same. His voice had a note of warmth that she had never noticed before, and his eyes held a gleam that promised much.

'It's lovely out here,' she sighed.

'Yes,' he murmured in her ear. 'It's lovely, and you're lovely.'

'You have to feel sorry for Romeo and Juliet, who could never take this kind of walk, just enjoying being together and letting the world drift by.'

'I guess we're luckier than they were.'

She turned to look up into his face. 'Yes,' she said. 'We're lucky. We were always lucky, if only we'd known it.'

His fingertips brushed her face gently. 'I always knew it,' he said. 'Now I know it even more since I had to endure life without you. I thought I'd never see you again, and the future was nothing but a terrible blank. But then

you were there again and I had my life back.
Suddenly, there was something to hope for.'

'Yes, for me too,' she said. 'But sometimes
I can be afraid to hope.'

'Better not to hope at all, than hope and
have it destroyed,' he said.

'No, I don't believe that. Wonderful things
can happen when you least expect it. You
have to be ready for the best as well as the
worst, and then— Oh, Mario, Mario!'

She was silenced by his mouth over hers.

'Be mine,' he whispered. 'Tell me that
you're mine.'

'I always was. I always will be.'

'Do you really mean that?'

'Yes—yes—'

'Say it again. Make me believe it.'

'I'm yours—all yours—yours—'

'For ever. I won't let you go. I warn you,
I'm possessive.'

'You couldn't be too possessive for me,'
she assured him.

His answer was another kiss which she returned with fervour.

A group of young people passed by, cheer-
ing and clapping at the sight of them.

'It's too public out here,' she said.

'Yes, let's go home.'

They slipped back into the hotel without

being seen. She was glad. What was happening now was for them alone.

He came with her as far as the apartment, then stopped at the door, regarding her uncertainly.

'Don't go,' she said, holding him in a gentle but determined hug. 'Stay with me.'

'Natasha, do you mean that?'

'Yes, I mean it.'

'But don't you realise that—if I stay—no, you don't realise. I mustn't stay.'

'Yes, you must,' she whispered. 'I say you must, and I won't let you refuse me.'

It hurt her to see how tense and vulnerable he seemed. After all the hostility that had simmered between them he couldn't believe that she was really opening her arms to him; even perhaps opening her heart. It was what he wanted but something he couldn't dare believe too easily, and she longed to reach out from her heart and reassure him.

'Trust me,' she murmured. 'Things move on. Nothing stays the same for ever.'

'Are you telling me that something really has changed?' he asked.

'In a way. I've learned to be more understanding. I was always so sure I was right, but now—now I feel like a different person. I have so much still to learn.'

She took a step back through the door, holding out her hand.

'Come in,' she said. 'Come with me—stay with me.'

He still could not understand her, but he put his hand in hers and followed her in perfect trust.

'Yes,' he said. 'Take me with you. Let me stay.'

His mouth was on hers, making her rejoice with heart, mind and body equally. There was pleasure but there was also a fierce possessiveness. She wanted him and she was determined to have him. She had waited as long as she could endure and now she was determined to enjoy her conquest.

With the door safely closed against the outside world, Mario felt able to yield to his longing and take her in his arms. Yet doubts and confusion still whirled about him.

'I don't believe this is happening,' he whispered. 'I've dreamed of it so often, so hopelessly.'

'Not hopelessly,' she told him. 'I've dreamed too. Dreams can come true. Let us believe that.'

'Yes, while I have you in my arms I can believe it.'

She drew his head down, kissing him with

fervour and passion, rejoicing in his response. Gradually he began to move towards the bed, easing her down onto it so that they lay together. When she felt him start to undo her clothes she was there before him, pulling open buttons, inviting him to explore her.

He accepted the invitation, tentatively at first, caressing her gently, almost uncertainly. But as his hands discovered the soft smoothness of her skin their touch became more fervent, more intense, sending tremors through her. She reached out to him, now working on his buttons so that his shirt fell open and she could explore him in her turn.

Once, long ago in Venice, she had dreamed of this. But fate had denied her dream, banishing her into a wilderness where there was no love, no hope, no Mario.

Now, at last, the moment had come and it was everything she'd wanted. His caress was tentative, almost as though he feared to touch her.

She understood. In the depths of her heart joy was warring with disbelief, scared that this might not really be true, that she would wake to find it a delusion. And it was the same with him. Instinct too deep for thought told her this was true. After so long their hearts and minds were as one, just as their bodies would soon unite.

He laid his face against her. She drew him closer, wanting this moment to last.

'Yes,' she murmured. 'Yes.'

'Yes,' he echoed. 'Natasha—are you sure?'

'I'm sure of everything—sure that I want you—'

He gave a faint smile. 'Are you sure I want you? Or shall I try to convince you?'

'I don't need convincing.' She returned his smile in full measure. 'But don't let me stop you.'

'Whatever you please, ma'am,' he murmured, intensifying his caresses.

Her pleasure rioted, but more than pleasure was the joy of knowing that they were close again. The man she had loved long ago had been stolen from her, but now she had him back. And she would never let him go again. The world might turn upside down. The heavens might fall, the seas overflow, but she would never release him from her arms and her heart. On that she was resolved.

He worked eagerly on her clothes until nothing was left. Then he removed his own garments and they were naked together. He took her into his arms, kissing her mouth, her face, her neck, then going lower to smother

her breasts in kisses. She took long breaths of delight at the storm growing within her, longing for the moment when he would claim her completely. When it came, it was everything she'd hoped.

CHAPTER NINE

As the fierce excitement died they lay quietly, holding each other, coming to terms with the new world in which they found themselves. Gradually they fell into peaceful sleep, lying motionless together until the room grew lighter and the new day had come.

Mario was lying with his face hidden against her neck, but then he raised it and looked down at her.

She met his eyes, seeing in them a look of loving possessiveness that made her heart skip a beat.

'Natasha,' he murmured, almost as though trying to believe that it was really her. She knew how he felt, for she was feeling the same herself. She had told him they must believe that dreams could come true.

'I've wanted this from the first moment,' he whispered. 'But I'd given up hope. And then suddenly—beyond my wildest dreams—why?'

'The time was right,' she whispered. 'Couldn't you feel that?'

'I've often felt it, but I was always wrong before. Suddenly—everything became different between us.'

'Everything became as it should be,' she said. 'This is how it was always meant to be.'

'You really mean that? Natasha, I'm not deluding myself, am I? Things are really all right between us?'

'How can you ask me that? After the way we've spent the last night, don't you think everything is all right?'

'Oh, yes.' He gave a wry smile. 'But I didn't mean that. I meant the other things that have come between us and separated us in the past. You didn't believe what I told you about Tania, that I'd broken with her because I'd met you and you were the one I wanted. Please, please say that you believe me, that you trust me at last.'

'I trust you, my darling. I should have trusted you long ago, but I was blind. It was like being lost in a maze. Every time I thought I'd found a way out it just led to more confusion.'

She promised herself that one day soon she would tell him about Tania's letter, and the way it had confirmed everything he said.

But she didn't want thoughts of Tania to intrude just now. She wanted only Mario, the warmth, beauty and contentment they could find together.

'You trust me,' he echoed as though trying to believe it. 'And you're mine.'

'I'm yours.'

'For always?'

'Always and for ever.'

'Then everything's perfect.'

'Not quite,' she said. 'Don't you have an "always and for ever" promise to make me?'

'Of course. I just didn't think you needed to hear it said. I'm so completely yours that—'

He was interrupted by the sound of his mobile phone. Sighing, he answered it, speaking in Italian. Natasha didn't understand the language, but she understood that the caller was Mario's brother, Damiano.

'Come stai, fratello?' Mario said cheerfully. *'Come è Sally e il bambino?'*

After listening a moment he gave Natasha a thumbs-up sign.

'They've set the christening for this weekend,' he told her. 'I'm going and they want me to take you.'

'They want me? But how—?'

'Yes or no?'

'Yes. Oh, yes.'

'Damiano—Natasha *dice di sì. Va bene!*'
He hung up.

'I don't understand,' she said. 'How did
they even think of inviting me?'

'You mean how did they know you were
here, and we'd found each other again?' He
became a little awkward. 'When I went there
for the birth a while ago I may have mentioned you briefly.'

She gave him a glance of wicked humour.
'Yes, I can imagine what you said. "That
pesky woman has turned up again, when I
thought I'd got rid of her."'

'Something like that,' he said with a grin.

'I'd give a lot to have been a fly on the wall.'

'You'd probably have had a good laugh. I
talked about you non-stop. When I told them
how amazed I was when our publicist turned
out to be you, Damiano roared with laughter.
And Sally wanted to know everything. She
thinks it's a great joke to see me conquered
by a woman.'

'But I haven't tried to conquer you.'

'Of course. If you had tried I'd have fought
back and we wouldn't be talking like this
now. But you caught me unaware, and I was
finished before I knew it.'

And before I knew it, she thought. His
words struck a disturbing chord within her.

'I remember everything so vividly,' he said. 'Our first meeting—you were sitting in the restaurant of Damiano's hotel when I came in. You were so lovely I just stopped and stared at you. Suddenly you looked up and saw me. And you smiled. Such a lovely smile, as though I was the only person in the room—in the world.

'I didn't understand straight away what had happened to me. But I did know that suddenly the world was focused on you.'

'And you came and sat down at the table,' she remembered. 'You said that you worked in the hotel and were offering your services—'

'That was just an excuse to talk to you, find out all I could about you. Were you married, was a man coming to join you? I hung on your every answer as though my life depended on it. And now I realise that my life did depend on it. And then—'

'What is it?' she asked, for he suddenly seemed troubled.

'It all happened again, didn't it? When you came here I asked you the same questions the first evening.'

'You said would a man turn up to drag me home?' she remembered.

'Yes, it sounded like the practical questions of an employer, but in fact I had this terrible need to know if there was someone in your life, just like the first time. It shocked me. I couldn't believe it had happened again—'

'With a woman you hated,' she said gently.

'I didn't hate you. I told myself I did because I needed to believe it. That was my defence and I clung to it. But things change and—well—'

'I wonder how much things change,' she murmured. 'Or do they only seem to have changed because *we* have changed?'

'Maybe we've changed in some things but not in others.'

'I wonder which is which.'

'We might find that out in Venice.'

'Mmm. So Sally thinks we're a joke. Yes, it's like fate played a joke on us. Sometimes I almost fancy I can hear laughter echoing from the heavens at the way we fell for it.'

'We didn't fall for it,' he said, drawing her close. 'We won. Fate lost. When Sally sees us together she'll understand that we're having the last laugh.'

'You really want me to come to Venice with you?'

'I think it's important that we go back there together.'

She understood. By returning they would confront their memories and that would help to show them the way forward.

'Everything that happened there looks different now,' she said.

'Yes,' he agreed gladly. 'So different. So much happier. The sooner we go the better. Then we can have a few days before the christening.'

At once he called Venice again, to say they would be arriving that evening. Then he stopped, regarding Natasha uneasily.

'Sally says one room or two?' he said. 'What's your choice?'

She was suddenly struck by inspiration. 'I'd like the same room I had last time.'

'That's a single room.'

'Perhaps we should be a little discreet.'

He seemed about to protest, but then understanding dawned and he turned back to the phone. At last he hung up.

'She's fixing it.'

'Does she think I'm crazy?'

'No, she said it made a lot of sense to put the clock back. I don't need to ask what that means, do I?'

'I don't think you do.'

'Let's get packing.'

Not long after, they bid farewell to Giorgio and set off for the Verona railway station to catch the train. It was just over seventy miles, and an hour and a half passed before they found themselves on the causeway that led over the water from the mainland to Venice.

She remembered the last time she had made this journey, leaning out of the window to see the beautiful buildings grow closer. How excited she'd been during that journey, how thrilled at the thought of spending time in the magical city.

At Venice station Mario hailed a water taxi and soon they were on their way to the hotel on the Grand Canal.

'There it is,' he said, pointing forward. 'Remember?'

'Yes, I remember,' she breathed.

It was a magnificent building, a converted palace that seemed to sum up everything that was glamorous about Venice. As soon as they entered Damiano and Sally came to meet them. Damiano and Mario slapped each other on the shoulders in brotherly fashion, while Sally embraced Natasha.

'It's lovely to see you again,' she said. 'And Pietro has really looked forward to your return. He says when you were last here you used to talk to him about football.'

'That's right. And last night England played Italy.' Natasha chuckled. 'Luckily, Italy won.'

Pietro appeared. He was in his early teens,

already looking strikingly like his father, and full of beans.

'Did you see the match?' he challenged at once, after which perfect communication was established between them.

'How's Toby?' she asked, meaning Pietro's spaniel, who had helped bring Damiano and Sally together.

'Here he is,' Pietro said eagerly, drawing his furry friend forward.

She greeted Toby, received his welcoming lick and looked up to find Mario watching them with a pleased smile, as though everything was working out as he'd hoped.

Then Sally took them to see the two children she'd borne her husband—little Franco, nearly three years old, whose birth had nearly cost her life, and Elena, the little girl she'd borne recently.

'Supper's in half an hour,' Sally said.

As promised, Natasha had the same room as before which, at first, gave her a slightly weird ghostly feeling. But it soon faded against the different, happier, reality of the present. Mario's room was just a few feet along the corridor, and soon he appeared to escort her downstairs to Damiano's private dining room.

It was clear to Natasha that she was being

welcomed into the family. During the meal that followed she was toasted as an honoured guest.

'Wait till you see the church where we'll have the christening,' Pietro said. 'It's where Mamma and Papà got married.'

'That was quite a ceremony,' Mario recalled. 'Toby was there too, practically one of the witnesses.'

'I'm sure he performed his role perfectly,' Natasha said.

As she spoke she tickled Toby's head and was rewarded with a *woof!*

It was a happy evening. A sense of peace came over her as she realised yet again the true purpose of this trip: to put right the mistakes and misunderstandings of the past.

Only Sally's brother Charlie was missing, which Sally explained with sisterly frankness. 'Out making himself objectionable again.'

'What kind of objectionable?' Natasha asked, laughing.

'Women, gambling—you name it, he can do it. Mind you, he's not as bad as he was. Mario helped reform him a bit.'

'Me? Reform?' Mario squeaked. 'That's practically an insult.'

'Well, Damiano told me you had a "guardian angel" side, and you did keep Charlie on the straight and narrow—more or less. Time for bed, anyway.'

The party broke up. Mario announced that he and Natasha wanted to take a walk. The others nodded in perfect understanding and slipped away.

'A walk?' she queried.

'Maybe. Maybe not.'

'What was the idea—?'

'I wanted to be sure of being alone with you. Let's have a coffee. Not here—in the restaurant.'

It was almost closing time and most of the restaurant tables were empty. At once she knew why he'd brought her here. There in the corner was the table where she'd sat at their first meeting. He led her over, showed her to a seat and sat beside her. A waiter brought them coffee.

'You were just here by the window,' he said. 'I watched you for a few minutes, trying to believe my eyes, rather like that guy over there.'

He pointed to a young man standing just inside the door, his eyes fixed on another table just a few feet away from them, where sat a young woman in her twenties. She was beautiful, and she was alone.

'I can guess what he's thinking,' Mario

said. 'He's working out a good excuse to approach her.'

'You can't know what he's thinking.'

'Oh, yes, I can. When I look at him I see myself. In fact, I see every guy trying to summon up the courage to approach a woman he knows is going to matter more than any other. Look, there he goes.'

As they watched, the young man approached the girl and gestured to ask if anyone was sitting with her. She shook her head and he took a seat.

'Does he work here?' Natasha asked.

'No, he'll have to think of another excuse. He doesn't seem to be doing too badly.'

Amused, they watched the couple for a few minutes. Then Mario said with a touch of unease, 'There's something I keep wanting to ask you.'

'What is it?'

He hesitated, then said, 'What happened to you after we parted? I know you worked hard and Jenson gave you a bad time, but was there—anything else?'

'You mean another man? But I've already told you about that.'

'You've told me you're not married, you haven't settled down with anyone, but that's not what I meant.'

She gave a gentle chuckle. 'You mean am I
secretly yearning for someone? Take a guess.'

'No, I can't see you yearning for someone
who didn't return the feeling. But surely in
the last two years you must have had some
sort of romantic interest.'

'No. Apart from the horrible Jenson I've
been alone. Which is a kind of freedom,' she
added wryly.

'I know exactly how that feels.'

'Don't tell me you've been alone,' she
teased. 'Every woman who passes gives you
yearning looks.'

'But what matters is to be wanted by the
one you yourself want,' he said. 'The others
don't count.'

'That's true,' she said softly.

'So you're telling me there was no other
man?'

'Hmm!' She appeared to consider this before saying gently, 'I suppose I could always
say that it's none of your business. How about
that?'

'It's certainly one response.' He gave her a
wry smile. 'I could go and bury myself under
the bedclothes because I couldn't cope with
you snubbing me. Or I could get blind drunk.
Or I could say that your lovers definitely are

my business. And always will be. So now what?'

His eyes met hers, gleaming with a mixture of humour and intensity that struck her to the heart.

'My lovers,' she mused. 'I wonder just what you've heard.'

'Not a thing. After you vanished I tried to hunt you down for a little while, but when you never made contact with me I thought—well—' He gave a slight shrug.

'You thought, "To hell with the silly English girl! If she wants to play it like that let her go and jump in the lake."'

'Well, maybe once or twice, but I didn't mean it,' he said, colouring.

'Oddly enough, I did end up in a lake shortly afterwards. It was a pleasure trip and the boat collapsed.'

'*What?* Were you hurt?'

'No, I just I got wet. Hey, I wonder if you made that happen. Strange to think we were in touch all that time and didn't know it.'

'Possibly. You were never off my mind.'

'Nor you off mine. And I did some cursing of my own.'

'I'm not sure I want to know about that,' he said with a grin. 'It could give me nightmares.'

'If we're asking about each other's lovers—what about yours? You must have had plenty.'

'Not lovers,' he said. 'Girlfriends, perhaps. I won't deny that I've enjoyed the company of a certain kind of woman because that way I could briefly forget the way you threw me overboard. But there wasn't anyone that I loved, even for a moment. It was always you, even when I most desperately didn't want it to be you.'

'Couldn't get rid of me, huh?' she teased.

'No matter how hard I tried.' He gave a warm laugh. 'You're a pesky woman. I told you a hundred times to get out of my heart but you just said, "Nope. Here I am and here I'm staying."'

'That sounds like me.'

He looked up suddenly. Following his gaze, she saw the other couple rise from the table and depart, hand in hand.

'I guess he got lucky,' Mario mused.

'Or maybe she did.'

'I didn't get lucky. Damiano called me to look after another customer and when I returned you'd gone. If only you could have heard me cursing.' He drained his coffee. 'Let's go.'

Upstairs, he came with her as far as her door. 'Remember last time?' he asked.

'Yes, we said goodnight at this door. I went inside and you went away.'

'I didn't really go away. I stayed out here in the corridor for ages.'

She opened the door and stretched out a hand to him.

'No need for that this time,' she said.

He took her hand at once, eagerly letting her draw him inside, then going into her arms, which she opened to him. It was she who drew them to the bed, he who followed her lead, but slowly, as though aware that they were rewriting history. Once they had wanted each other without satisfaction. Now they embraced satisfaction eagerly, joyfully.

There was physical pleasure in their caresses, but more than that was the joy of rediscovering each other. To retread the road, each seeing the other with new eyes, exploring new diversions, making wonderful discoveries; these were things they had never dared to dream of.

Afterwards, as they lay together in each other's arms, Natasha gave a sudden soft chuckle.

'What is it?' he demanded. 'What did I do that makes you laugh?'

'Don't get defensive. You could make me laugh and still be "macho".'

She laughed again and he frowned, demanding, 'So what is it?'

'It's what Sally said about you having a "guardian angel" side. That's the last thing I'd ever have suspected about you. A rebel, a pain in the butt, a pesky clown—any of them. But a guardian angel? Or any kind of angel. I doubt it.'

His annoyance faded and he kissed her forehead. 'Thanks. I see you really understand me.'

'You don't mind being called those things?'

'Not at all. I'd have minded being called an angel. That would have been insulting. But I think "pain in the butt" rather suits me.'

'Definitely,' she said, kissing him. 'Now, I'm going to sleep. You've exhausted me for the night. Goodnight, "guardian angel".'

She snuggled against him and in a few moments she was asleep.

Guardian angel, he thought. *That's almost funny, considering how I hated you only recently. But somehow things took a different turn.*

He rested his head against her and in a few minutes he too was asleep. After several hours he awoke to find her eyes still closed and her head on his shoulder. When he ventured to move slightly her arms tightened, as though even in sleep she needed to keep him close.

He clasped her back, offering her the embrace she needed for reassurance.

Romeo's words drifted through his mind again. *It is my lady...oh, it is my love. Oh, that she knew she were.*

But she does know, he mused. *If she knows anything by now, it's that I love her.*

He kissed her gently, murmuring, 'You are my lady. You are my love.'

She sighed and nestled closer, smiling as though she'd heard him and been reassured. He leaned against her, happy and willing to sleep again, but then a noise from his phone disturbed him.

'Curses,' he muttered. 'My mobile phone. Where is it?'

Undressing hastily, he hadn't noticed it fall to the floor. Now he eased himself gently away from Natasha and leaned down to pick up the phone. Connecting, he found a text from an unknown number:

You're taking a bigger risk than you know. She's mine. Get lost.

For a moment he was simply bewildered. Who could the message be from? But then the answer came to him like a clap of thunder.

Elroy Jenson. The man who'd vindictively

destroyed Natasha's career because she'd dared to defy him. The man who'd spied on her from a distance, watching where she fled to escape him. The man who still had his claws in her, and would deepen them if he could.

He was swept by such rage that his head was dizzy and the whole world seemed to turn black.

'No,' he whispered. 'She's not yours. She's mine. She's *mine*. She always was. *And she always will be.*'

Behind him, Natasha stirred, murmuring, 'Is something the matter?'

'No,' he said. 'Go back to sleep. Nothing's the matter. Nothing at all. Your guardian angel will deal with it.'

CHAPTER TEN

'HOW ARE YOU enjoying Verona?' Sally asked Natasha at breakfast next morning.

'I love it.'

'And Verona loves her,' Mario said. 'She's doing a great job for our hotels.'

'Perhaps she can come here later and do something for Venice hotels,' Damiano said.

'What a lovely idea,' Natasha said. 'I'll take a stroll around Venice this morning.' She glanced at Mario before saying slowly, 'Just to remind myself what it's like.'

He nodded.

After breakfast they slipped out into the narrow alley that ran by the hotel.

'You walked this way alone the first time,' he reminded her. 'But I wasn't far behind you.'

'I know.'

'You know? You mean you knew it then?'

'Yes, I told the receptionist where I was

going, and you were nearby. When I came out I heard your footsteps behind me.'

'So you always knew I was following you?'

'No, but I hoped you were. I went into a shop to give you a chance to catch up. But you didn't.'

'I was tempted. When you stopped I worked out a plan to go into the shop casually and just "happen" to meet you. But I lost my nerve, so I waited a bit.'

'Lost your nerve? You?'

'You have that effect on me.'

'I'll remember that. It could be useful.'

'Be honest. You already knew that you scared me stiff.'

Laughing, they went on their way.

At last they came to the Grand Canal, the great S-shaped stream of water that wound through the city. Boats of every kind filled it. Just coming up was a *vaporetto*, one of the great water buses that transported passengers all over the city. Small water taxis were everywhere, but also the boats that everyone came to Venice to see, gondolas. Natasha looked eagerly at the slim, elegant conveyances, propelled by a man with one oar.

'You were standing here when you saw your first gondola close up,' he remembered.

'And I couldn't think how a gondola could

go straight when it was only being rowed on one side,' she said. 'You told me that that side bulged more than the other, so the water took longer to slide past. I didn't understand, so you said I should take a ride in it. You hailed the gondolier—like you're doing now.'

The boat was gliding to a halt beside them. Gently, he handed her in and they settled down together. It felt wonderful, just as it had the first time.

'Aaaaaah.' Sighing with pleasure, she stretched out, looking around her at the little canal and listening to the singing coming from around the corner. 'It's lovely, but this is where I fell asleep.'

'That's right. You couldn't have made it plainer what you thought of me, Natasha— Natasha?'

She was lying back with her eyes closed. *Just like last time*, he thought.

The gondolier regarded him sympathetically. 'Some men are just unlucky, *signore*,' he said, speaking in Venetian dialect.

'True,' Mario said wryly in the same language. 'But some men are also luckier than they know. The problem is finding out which you are.'

He watched Natasha carefully for a moment, then leaned forward and kissed her.

When she didn't react he repeated the kiss more forcefully.

'Hello,' Natasha said, opening her eyes.

'Hello. Sorry if I disturbed you.'

'Tell me, when I fell asleep the first time, did you kiss me then?'

'Don't you remember?'

She smiled up at him in a way he guessed was meant to drive him mad. She was certainly succeeding. Did she know that? Did she enjoy it?

'I'm not sure,' she murmured.

'Then let me remind you.'

He laid his lips gently over hers again, leaving them there for several moments.

The gondolier grinned. His job exposed him to a lot of enjoyable sights.

Natasha relaxed and put her arms about him. Although she had been asleep for their first ride, two years ago, she was sure he hadn't kissed her then because she would have remembered. Now she gave herself up to pleasure.

Afterwards, they sat leaning against each other, watching the little canals drift past. She had a mysterious sense that the journey might go on for ever, and wished that it would. But all too soon they drew up outside the hotel. Once inside, they became involved in the preparations for the christening, and for the rest of the day she barely spent a moment alone with him.

Next morning everyone set out for the church where the christening would take place. It was only a short distance away, so they went on foot.

'It's a big family occasion,' Mario said as they walked through the alley that approached the church. 'Damiano's first wife died giving birth to Pietro. One reason he married Sally was to give that kid a mother.'

'You mean it was a marriage of convenience? They seem so devoted to each other.'

'They are. They thought it was a marriage of convenience, but in fact they were really in love. They just hadn't realised it.'

She looked into her wine glass, murmuring, 'That can happen when people don't understand their own feelings.'

'So I've heard. It must be quite a stunning discovery.'

'Yes,' she said. 'It is. There's no recovering from it, or from blaming yourself for how stupid you were.'

'Would you call yourself stupid?'

'Mad, imbecile,' she said. 'Even worse than

that. But a lucky fate gave me the chance to put things right.'

He raised his glass. 'Here's to fate.'

They clinked glasses.

'So did they realise they were in love?' she asked.

'It dawned on them eventually. She had a bad time when Franco was born. She might not have come through it. I thought Damiano would go out of his mind with fear and grief. He wasn't keen on Sally having another baby, but she really wanted it and he gave in.'

He gave a brief laugh. 'Few people know the real Damiano. To the outside world he's a ruthless businessman. But once that front door shuts behind him, he's a willing slave to his wife.'

'Oh, really?' She gave him a cheeky look. 'Is that how you judge a good husband? If he's her willing slave?'

'Who knows? Perhaps you'll have the chance to find out.'

There were already plenty of friends and family in place, smiling when they appeared and made their way along the aisle. Sally walked with her new baby in her arms, Damiano carried their toddler, Charlie and Mario walked together, while Pietro accompanied

Natasha, holding her hand. Again she had the happy feeling of being part of the family.

It grew even better at the party that evening. Mario introduced her to everyone in the crowd, most of whom seemed to have heard of her already.

'We've all looked forward to meeting you,' said one elderly man.

'Just be a little patient,' Mario told him. 'You'll hear something soon.'

'What did that mean?' she asked as he drew her away.

'Just that people think we're a couple. Do you mind that?'

'Not at all,' she assured him. 'But what is he going to hear soon?'

'Why don't we go and talk about that?'

He drew her slowly out of the room, waving farewell to the other guests, who cheered them in a way that left no doubt that they were expecting to hear about a wedding very soon. Somehow, Mario had given that impression.

Once inside her room he kissed her before saying, 'I may have said more than I should have done without asking you first. But we so clearly belong together that people accept it.'

'And if you could have asked me first?'

'I'd have asked you to set the date for our wedding.'

'Yes, you really should have mentioned it to me.'

'Are you mad at me?'

'I'll let you know that later.' She drew him to the bed. 'For the moment I have other things on my mind.'

'So have I.' He was already working on her clothes.

We did the right thing coming here, she thought. *It's made things better, as nothing else could have done. The past is over. It didn't happen. We are free.*

Free. The word seemed to echo, casting hope over the future. As they made love she kept her eyes on his face, finding that he too was watching her, sending a silent message that she understood and returned with all her heart.

And he too understood. She recognised that from the long sigh of happiness and fulfilment he gave as they lay in each other's arms afterwards.

'If only we could have known,' he whispered.

'It was too much to hope for,' she replied. 'Even now I daren't hope. It's too good to be true. Something will happen to make things go wrong.'

'Nothing will go wrong,' he said firmly. 'I won't let it.'

'Oh, you think it's all up to you, do you, big man?'

'Right this minute I feel powerful enough to dictate everything in the world. You hear that?' he yelled up at the ceiling. 'Nothing is ever going to go wrong between us again. I insist on it. I order it.'

'Who are you giving orders to?' she chuckled.

'The little green men who try to dictate to us. From now on, I'm in charge.'

'Oh, yeah?'

'Not of you,' he said hastily. 'Just of them.'

They collapsed with laughter, rocking back and forth with delight.

Afterwards, Natasha was to remember that moment, a triumphant assertion of joy and confidence before catastrophe descended on them once more.

Next morning Mario suggested a walk through Venice.

'It was a good idea to come back,' he said as they strolled. 'The people we were then don't exist any more, and this way we've got rid of them.'

'I'm not sure I want to get rid of them,' she observed. 'There were things about you I think I'll cling to. You've always been the best-looking man for miles around. I'm not changing that.'

'Thank you, ma'am.'

He began to draw her in another direction, but she resisted.

'Why can't we stay here?' she asked.

'Because of that place,' he said, indicating an outdoor café. It was the one where they had had their quarrel.

But it need not have happened, she thought.

So many times she'd wanted to tell Mario that she knew the truth after reading Tania's letter, but somehow the moment had never been right. But perhaps this was the right time and place.

'Why don't you buy me a coffee there?' she said.

'Don't you realise what that place is?' he demanded.

'Yes, it's where we made our huge mistake and lost each other. Perhaps it's time to put it right.'

'I thought we'd already put it right.'

'Yes, but there's a little more to do. Come with me.'

She led him to the café and found that by a strange chance the same table was available.

'This is where we sat,' she said as they sipped coffee.

'Until we were interrupted, but that won't happen this time,' he said firmly. 'That woman is out of our lives for good.' He became suddenly tense. 'What's the matter? Why are you smiling like that? Don't you believe me?'

'Yes, I believe you.'

'Do you really? You believe that I was telling you the truth? You trust me? I would never deceive you. Tell me that you believe that.'

'I do. I believe everything you've told me. I know you're an honest man and you always will be.'

'You mean that? You really mean that?'

'Every word.'

He took her face between his hands and spoke softly. 'If you could imagine what it means to me to know that we're close enough for you to have learned to trust me.'

'I only want to tell you—' She stopped, silenced by a nervous feeling that she did not understand.

'You only want to tell me what? That you love me. That's it, isn't it?'

'Oh, yes, that's it.'

'Then that's all I need to hear.'

'But, Mario—'

His lips on hers silenced her. He was kissing her fiercely, powerfully, yet devotedly, longingly. She surrendered to the pleasure, knowing that this, and only this, was the whole of life.

At last he released her. She could tell that he was shaking and his breath came unevenly.

'My darling,' he whispered. 'What is it that you needed to say?'

'Nothing. It doesn't matter.'

Nothing mattered enough to break the spell of this moment. She took hold of him again, returning the kiss fervently. Around them the other diners laughed and cheered, and the waiter cleared his throat. Without looking at him, Mario pulled some money from his pocket. The waiter seized it and vanished.

'Let's go,' Mario said. 'This isn't the place for what we have to do.'

'*Have* to do?' she murmured against his lips.

'We have urgent business to attend to,' he whispered. 'Can't you feel it?'

'Yes—oh, yes.'

Seizing her hand, he rose and hurried away. She followed him joyfully. The words she'd planned to say could wait. Nothing mattered now but to be with him, in his arms, his bed, his life.

Together they ran through the streets of Venice, down alleys, over bridges, eager to get to the hotel, where they could achieve the fulfilment that awaited them, that they longed for.

At last they reached the hotel, hurrying through the entrance and across to the lift.

Sally appeared, calling, 'Ah, Mario, can I talk to you—?'

'Not now,' Mario called back.

They vanished into the lift, clinging to each other as it carried them up.

'Nearly there,' he said hoarsely.

'Yes, nearly there.'

She knew he meant they were almost at his bedroom, but to her the words meant far more. The glorious destination that had waited for them since the moment they'd met—they were nearly there.

They had reached the room. He flung open the door, drew her inside and began to undress her at once. She responded instantly, wrenching off his jacket, pulling open his buttons, tearing off his shirt.

They fell onto the bed, still working on each other's clothes until they were both naked and ready for each other.

'You're mine,' he said huskily. 'Now and for ever.'

'Yes—yes—'

She was dizzy with passion and delight, wanting him more than she had ever wanted anything in her life. Their previous lovemaking had been wonderful, but this one was pervaded by an extra sense of triumph.

She reached for him, offered herself to him, claimed him, and sensed his delight not only through his movements but by the glow in his eyes. His lovemaking was tender, emotional, and at first this was enough. But soon she wanted more. She was his, heart and body, and with every movement she demanded that he accept the gift and return it. When he claimed her finally she cried out with joy.

Afterwards, lying contentedly in his arms, feeling the warmth of his flesh and the gentle power of his embrace, she knew that she had come to the place that was always meant for her, and where she could live happily for the rest of her life.

She had meant to tell him about the letter, but things beyond her control had swept her up. Was that an omen? she wondered. Should she try to tell him now?

'My love,' she murmured.

'My love,' he echoed, 'if you knew how wonderful it is to hear you call me that. I am your love and you are mine.' He stroked her breast. 'I was afraid this would never happen,' he whispered.

'It's not the first time we've made love,' she reminded him.

'No, but it's the first time we've made love like this, with all doubts settled, all fears gone, everything open and clear between us. When you told me that you trusted me I felt as if I'd gone to heaven.'

'Yes,' she whispered. 'I feel like that too.'

'And we must keep it that way. We lost two years, but we mustn't lose any more time. We must marry as soon as possible.'

'Marry,' she said in wonder.

'I told you yesterday that we should set the date. You didn't give me an answer. Are you trying to put me off?'

She glanced down the bed at their naked entwined figures. 'Does it look as if I'm trying to put you off?'

'I just want to be sure of you. Say yes. Say yes.'

'Oh, yes. Yes, with all my heart.'

'Now we've found each other,' he whispered, 'nothing can ever come between us.'

He kissed her again before saying, 'I've just remembered—you had something you were trying to say to me.'

'Did I?'

'Yes, it sounded urgent but I kind of distracted you.' He grinned, recalling the way he'd grasped hold of her and made her run.

'I suppose you could call this a distraction,' she agreed, smiling.

'So what were you going to say?'

Natasha's head was whirling. This was the moment she'd planned to lay bare the secret, but suddenly everything seemed different. To speak of it now would be to let Tania intrude on them again, and she was determined never to let that happen.

'Natasha?' he murmured.

'Mmm?'

'Are you awake?'

'Er…no. I—must have dozed off again. Did you say something?'

'I asked you what you'd been planning to tell me.'

'I can't remember. It's gone out of my head now, so it can't have meant much.'

'It's just that you made it sound important.'

'No, it couldn't be.' She touched his face. 'Only one thing is important now.'

'And that's us,' he agreed. 'You're right. Nothing else matters. Come here.'

She did so, taking refuge in his arms and his love, so that the rest of the world ceased to exist.

The letter didn't matter, she decided. This was how it would always be.

She opened her eyes next morning to find Mario regarding her anxiously.

'You did mean it, didn't you?' he asked. 'You really will marry me?'

'No,' she teased. 'I was just making fun of you. Oh, don't look like that. Of course I meant it. Would I have said it otherwise?'

'I can't be sure with you. You always seem to have a surprise to spring on me. I get nervous waiting for the next one.'

'Oh, really?' She regarded him with wicked humour. 'Let's see now. I could always thump you.'

'But that wouldn't be a surprise. You've already thumped me so often in different ways.'

'So maybe it's time to find another way. How about that?' She delivered a light pat on his shoulder.

'Ouch!' he cried comically. 'Now I'm in agony.'

'Good. Then I'll know how to bully you in future.'

She patted him again and they both burst into laughter.

'I don't believe this is real,' he said against her neck. 'Nobody could be as happy as I am now. It's an illusion.'

'No, we're going to teach the world what happiness looks like.'

'Mmm, that sounds nice. Can I thump you back?'

'Permission granted.'

He rolled her onto her stomach and lightly patted her behind. 'You be careful,' he said, 'or I'll do it again.'

'Is that a promise?' she chuckled.

'It's whatever you want.'

He was right, she thought, nestling contentedly against him. Nobody was allowed to be as happy as this. It must be an illusion. And she would do everything in her power to make it last.

CHAPTER ELEVEN

ENTERING THE BREAKFAST room downstairs, they found Damiano, Sally and Pietro waiting for them. They all looked up, eager for news.

'Have you got something to tell us?' Damiano asked. 'Sally seemed to think you might have.'

'You mean after she tried to talk to me yesterday and we dashed upstairs?' Mario said. 'Sorry, Sally. It was urgent.'

'Well, I gathered that,' she chuckled. 'So come on, tell us.'

'We're going to be married,' he announced. 'Natasha has decided she can put up with me.'

Pietro cried, 'Yippee!'

Sally hugged Natasha, and Damiano declared cheerfully, 'Welcome to the family, Natasha. We're all delighted that you're going to take charge of Mario and turn him into a sensible man.'

'Thanks, brother,' Mario said, grinning.

'By the time you discover your mistake it'll be too late,' Mario added. 'He'll have put the ring on your finger.'

'And I'll never let her take it off,' Mario said.

'You must marry here in Venice,' Sally said. 'After all, it's where you met. It'll be such fun to arrange.'

'That's very nice of you,' Mario said, 'but I think there's another place that would be more right for us. In Verona, we can marry at Juliet's house.' He glanced at Natasha, who nodded, smiling.

'Romeo and Juliet,' Sally mused. 'But you two can't be Romeo and Juliet. You're having a happy ending. I suppose there's still time for something to go wrong, but it won't.'

'No, it won't,' Mario said. 'We're together, and now nothing is going to go wrong. She is my Juliet, and Verona is the right place for us.'

Sally insisted on having a party for them that evening. Her warmth was a special blessing to Natasha. Her life had been lonely, with no relatives but her bitter mother. Now, suddenly, she had a brother and sister, and a cheeky nephew in Pietro.

They laughed and danced their way through the party, spent the night nestled together, and set out for Verona the following morning.

When Giorgio heard the news he roared with delight.

'Romeo and Juliet made it at last! What a story.'

'It's not exactly a story,' Mario protested.

'It is to me. You hired me as your publicity manager, and I'm going to do my job. When you've fixed the date we'll get some pictures.'

'The date will be as soon as possible,' Mario said.

'It'll have to be a Monday morning,' Giorgio told him. 'All wedding ceremonies are held then because the house has to be closed to tourists while it's happening. Then we'll have the reception here in the afternoon, and everyone in the *Comunità* will come.'

Later that day they went to the City Hall to make the booking for two weeks' time, and learned what they could about the wedding procedure. The actual ceremony would take place inside the building, with photographs taken afterwards, on the balcony.

Giorgio was in his element, planning to broadcast the information as far and wide as possible.

'This isn't just a wedding,' he said gleefully. 'It's the biggest publicity opportunity the *Comunità* has ever had. You really must make the best of it.'

'That's fine,' Mario said. 'I'm happy for everyone to know that I've secured the best bride in the world.'

But Natasha drew him aside, feeling some concern. 'Jenson will get to hear of it,' she said.

'Good!' Mario declared at once. 'I want him to know that his bullying has achieved nothing. That should stop his nonsense.'

'But suppose it doesn't?'

'Then I'll make him sorry he was born. Don't tell me you're still afraid of him. You're going to be my wife. There's nothing more he can do.' He took her in his arms. 'Trust me, darling. You have nothing more to fear from him. I told you I'd scare the living daylights out of him, and I have.'

'You scared Jenson? But how?'

'By slashing his advertising revenue. There are several media outlets I've been able to persuade to drop their adverts. Some here, some owned by friends of mine elsewhere. It should be enough to put the wind up him.'

'You did that for me?' she breathed. 'Oh, thank you—thank you.'

Blazing with happiness, she threw her arms around his neck.

'I told you I wouldn't let you be hurt,' he said. 'And I won't.'

'So you really are my guardian angel?'

'Angel? Not me. But I can put the wind up people when I want to.'

Chuckling, they embraced each other.

'It's such a weight off my mind,' she said. 'To know that he won't trouble me again.'

Now her most urgent arrangement was choosing a wedding dress. At Giorgio's orders, several gowns were delivered to the hotel for her to try on. She chose one of white satin, cut simply and elegantly.

'Perfect,' Giorgio declared when he saw it. 'It'll look great in the pictures. We must get started on them quickly.'

It seemed strange to be taking wedding pictures before the wedding, but they were to be part of Giorgio's publicity campaign to promote Verona as a wedding venue.

'The photographer will be here tomorrow morning,' Giorgio said. 'He's the same one who took the pictures of you as Romeo and Juliet. We'll put the two sets of pictures out together. Romeo and Juliet became Mario and Natasha.' He grinned. 'Or perhaps they always were.'

'Forget it,' Mario said. 'This story isn't going to end in a tomb.'

He was looking so handsome, Natasha thought as they posed together. For one picture she stood just in front of him, his hands on her shoulders as they both faced the camera. For another shot they danced together.

'Don't look so stern,' Giorgio called. 'Gaze into each other's eyes. Look romantic.'

'But why?' Natasha teased. 'We're getting married. 'That's not romantic; it's deadly serious.'

'Stop that,' Mario said. 'I'm quite scared enough without you scaring me more.'

She began to laugh. He joined in and Giorgio yelled with delight at the picture it produced.

'That's perfect,' he said. 'That says it all.'

As he'd predicted, the two sets of pictures worked splendidly together. When circulated to the rest of the *Comunità*, they produced a flood of excited congratulations.

There was one reaction Mario vowed to keep to himself. The text from Jenson was as spiteful as he'd expected, and he was thankful that Natasha didn't see it.

I've warned you but you didn't take any notice. Now see how sorry I can make you.

He checked the phone number of Jenson's organisation and dialled it.

'I want to speak to Elroy Jenson,' he told the receptionist.

'I'm sorry. Mr Jenson isn't accepting calls today.'

'He'll accept mine. Tell him Mario Ferrone wants to talk to him.'

A pause, some clicks, then a harsh masculine voice came on the line. 'What do you mean by calling me?'

'Ah, Mr Jenson. Good.' Mario leaned back in his chair. 'You know exactly who I am. You don't like me, and you're going to like me even less when I've finished.'

'You're wasting your time,' Jenson's voice came down the line.

'I don't think so. I think you'll find that some of my recent actions have been very significant.'

'What recent actions?' Jenson's voice contained a sneer but Mario thought he also detected a hint of nervousness.

'You'll be hearing from your Italian publications, wondering why whole batches of advertising have been suddenly cancelled.'

'Don't think you can scare me,' Jenson snapped. 'A few hotels and vineyards—'

'It'll be rather more than that. I've got friends working on this, friends you know nothing about but whose tentacles stretch great distances abroad. You'll be losing advertisements left, right and centre. And when they want to know why—I wonder what you'll tell them.'

'That's no concern of yours!' Jenson raged.

'Everything that concerns my fiancée concerns me, as you'll find out if you don't stop your nasty ways. You wrecked her career out of spite because she wasn't interested in your cheap advances and too many people got to know about it. Well, now the whole world is going to know about it.'

'What do you mean?' Jenson snarled.

'The digital age is a wonderful thing. A few texts and emails and the world will know what a pest Elroy Jenson is: a man so conceited that he felt no woman had the right to reject him, and with so little self-respect that he could never leave her alone afterwards.'

'There are laws of libel,' Jenson snarled.

'There's no question of libel. Once those texts you've sent her are revealed there would be no question everyone will know the truth.'

'Texts? I don't know what you're talking about.'

'Don't waste time trying to deny it. I've got records of every word you sent, and where they came from. I can reveal every word and prove it. The world will rock with laughter at you. And if you resorted to law you'd just keep yourself in an unpleasant spotlight longer.'

'What are you after? Money?'

'No, I just want you to leave Natasha alone. One more text or call from you and you've had it. Do you understand me?'

'You're very good at making threats,' Jenson snapped with his best effort at a sneer.

Mario grinned, feeling that he could risk a little vulgarity.

'I'm good at a lot of things,' he said. 'Which is why she chose me over you.'

'Why, you—'

'Goodbye. Go to hell!'

Mario hung up. Then he stared at the phone, trying to come to terms with his own actions. He was neither a violent nor a cruel man, but the need to conquer Jenson had brought out a side of him he'd never needed to use before.

But it was for her, and for her he would do anything. That was the effect she had on him, and now he realised that part of him had known it from the first day.

From behind him he heard a sound that made him turn in amazement. Natasha stood there, applauding.

'Well done,' she said. 'Wonderful! You've really dealt with him.' She engulfed him in an embrace.

'It was easy—just threaten to expose him as an idiot,' he said, returning her hug. 'He's far more afraid of that than losing business.'

'But I don't understand what you said about his texts. Surely you don't really have records of them?'

'Only the one he sent today. I don't have the others, but he doesn't know that and he won't take the chance.'

'No, he won't,' she breathed.

'And he won't dare send you any more because now he knows the risk he runs.'

'You're so clever.' She sighed. 'I never thought anyone could put this business right.'

'But you've got me to protect you now. And that's all I want to do for the rest of my life.'

He enfolded her in a fierce embrace.

'Three days before we're married,' he said huskily. 'I don't know if I can bear to wait that long to make you mine.'

'But I'm already yours. I always have been and I always will be.'

'No doubt about that,' he said, smiling. 'I'll never let you go.'

'That suits me just fine.'

Now things were moving fast. Two days before the wedding, Damiano, Sally and Pietro arrived and took up residence in the hotel's best suite. That evening there was a party attended by them, by Giorgio and by several members of the *Comunità*. Toasts were made to the bride and groom. Then the bride alone was toasted, leaving no doubt that she was the heroine of the hour.

As the evening wore on, Sally announced that she would retire for the night.

'I've got a bit of a headache,' she confided to Natasha.

'Me too,' she said. 'And I think Mario might enjoy chatting if he didn't have to keep breaking off to translate for me.'

Together they bid everyone goodnight and went upstairs. A warm, friendly hug and they said goodnight.

Natasha was glad to be alone for a moment for she needed to think. She must decide what to do about Tania's letter.

There had been a time when she might have told Mario about it but events had conspired to distract her and now she knew the moment had gone. Her best course now was to destroy it so that it would be out of their lives finally and for ever.

Going quickly into her room, she went to the place where she kept it hidden.

She found the small piece of blue paper and unfolded it.

She read it again, taking in the words that had meant so much, thanking a merciful fate that had given it to her. Now she reckoned she must burn it.

'What's that?' said Mario's voice.

Startled, she looked up and saw him there. He had come in quietly, without her hearing him. Now he was standing with his eyes fixed on the blue paper that she held. With dismay, she realised that he knew what she was holding.

'What's that?' he repeated.

'It's just—'

'Give it to me.'

He wrenched it from her hand before she could protest. As he read it he seemed to grow very still.

'How did you get this?' he asked in a toneless voice.

'By accident. I came across it while I was in your apartment, after my room flooded.'

'And you kept it.'

'I needed to read it again and again. It seemed too good to be true. She says there that you'd told her it was over because you wanted to be with me. So after that I knew—'

'You knew I'd been telling you the truth,' he said slowly.

'Yes. It was so wonderful. After everything that happened, who could have thought it would be Tania who would make things right for us?'

There was a silence.

When he spoke he didn't look at her. 'Did she make things right for us?' he asked in a strange voice.

'She added the missing piece. She told me what I needed to know. After that, everything was different.'

If only he would smile and share her pleasure at the way things had turned out, but instead he was silent, frowning. It was almost as though her words troubled him.

'Tell me something,' he said at last. 'That night we took a walk by the river and when we got home you invited me into your room— had you read Tania's letter then?'

'Yes. I was so happy. Suddenly everything was all right.'

'Why? Because Tania had confirmed I was telling the truth? You knew that because *she* told you? But not because *I* told you?'

'I didn't know you as well in those days. I couldn't be sure what the truth might be. Oh, Mario, why didn't you show me the letter yourself?'

'I meant to. But I was waiting for the right moment.'

'But surely any time would have been right to show me the proof?'

'The proof?'

'The proof that what you were telling me was true. That you really had broken with her.'

A strange, tense look came over his face. 'So you could have believed me when you saw proof. But not my word alone.'

'Mario, I'm sorry about that. I see now that I should have believed you. But does it matter now that it's been finally settled?'

'Settled.' He repeated the word softly. 'If only I could make you understand—'

'Understand what, my darling?'

'Since you came to Verona I've clung to a happy fantasy, a dream world in which we understood each other. In that world we grew close, loving each other more and more until you finally believed what I told you because you knew me well enough to know that I was true to you.'

'But I do know—'

'Yes, because you've got the evidence in that letter. But in my fantasy you didn't need evidence. You believed me because you loved me enough to trust me completely. We were so close that no doubt could ever come between us.

'That night, when you opened your arms to me, I felt I'd reached heaven. I thought our great moment had arrived at last, the moment I'd been longing for since the day we met. If only you knew how I... Well, never mind. It doesn't matter now.'

'But it does,' she cried passionately. 'Mario, don't talk like this. You sound as though everything is hopeless between us, but it isn't. We've discovered our hope at last. It's taken too long but we've finally found each other. Can't you see that?'

'I want to. If you knew how desperately I long to believe that everything can be all right now, but there's something missing and perhaps it always will be.'

She stared at him, struggling to believe what he was saying.

'Then blame me,' she said. 'I got it wrong; I took too long to understand the truth. But I understand it now.'

'Yes, because someone else told you. Not me. The closeness I thought we'd achieved doesn't exist. It was an illusion I believed because I wanted to believe it.' He gave a grim laugh. 'I remember you saying people believed what they wanted to, and boy were you right! In you I saw what I wanted to see.

'And now? Will we ever have that closeness? I doubt it. You said things were "finally settled". But when is something settled? When you finally have peace of mind?'

And now he did not have peace of mind with her. He didn't say it—but he didn't need to say it. She had thought that all was well between them, but after this would their love ever be the same?

'Do you understand the bitter irony of this?' he asked. 'The next thing is our wedding. We'll stand side by side at a site that commemorates the greatest lovers of legend. We'll vow love, loyalty, trust. *Trust!* Can you imagine that?'

'I do trust you,' she cried passionately.

'Do you? Perhaps you do, perhaps you don't. I'll never really know, will I?'

'Can't you take my word for it?'

He gave a harsh laugh. 'Are you lecturing me about accepting your word? That's the cruellest joke you ever made. I was looking forward to our wedding. Now I'm dreading it. I'm not even sure that I—'

He broke off, almost choking. His eyes, fixed on her, were full of hostility. Suddenly he turned, pulled open the door and rushed out without a backward glance.

'Mario—don't. Come back, *please.*'

But either he didn't hear or he ignored

her, heading for the stairs and running down them. At the bottom he turned towards the entrance. Dashing back into the room, Natasha went to the window and looked down, where she could see him heading down the street until he vanished.

She almost screamed in her despair. The perfect love that offered a wonderful future had descended into chaos. Now a terrifying vista opened before her. Ahead stretched a road of misery, where every hope came to nothing and only emptiness remained.

CHAPTER TWELVE

WHAT FOLLOWED WAS the worst night of Natasha's life.

It was over. Everything was over. She had lost Mario and nothing could ever matter in her life again.

Why didn't I tell him earlier? her heart cried.

But she knew the answer. However he had learned about the letter, he would have hated the fact that she'd relied on it. In his heart he no longer believed that she loved him. And now everything might be over between them. He had even hinted that he might not be there for the wedding.

For a moment she thought of chasing after him, but he'd had time to disappear and she would never find him. Her best hope was to wait for him to return.

She lay down, trying to control her wild thoughts and believe that there might still be hope. For an hour she lay there, listening for some sign of his return, but all she heard was the party breaking up.

Then there was silence and darkness, leaving her with an aching heart and terrified thoughts.

Why didn't he return?

Would he ever return?

She slept for a while and awoke in the early hours. There was no sign of Mario, but perhaps he'd gone to his own room. She slipped out into the corridor and went to his door, where she stood listening for a moment. But there was no sound from within.

Tentatively, she opened the door and slipped inside. The bed was empty. He had not returned.

'Come back,' she whispered. 'Don't let it end like this. Come back to me.'

But another two hours passed with no sign of him.

A terrible sense of irony pervaded her. Suddenly it felt as though she was Juliet again, a star-crossed lover facing the final destruction of her joy.

There was nothing to prepare her for what happened next.

A shrill from her mobile phone made her

look to find a text. Incredibly, it was from Jenson.

You think you're clever, setting your lover on me. Take a look at this.

Below it was the address of a website. Studying it, Natasha realised that it was an English provincial newspaper, doubtless belonging to Jenson.

He'd said he knew something about her, implying that he could smear her in print. But she couldn't think of anything she would be reluctant to have known.

She got to work on her laptop, typing in the web address. There on the screen was a printed page with a photograph. A cry broke from her as she recognised her father.

Forcing herself under control, she looked closely at the text. It was dated eight years ago and named the man as Charles Bates. It seemed to be part of a series about people who had been brought down by misfortune. Charles Bates had turned to crime and gone to prison following a tragic crisis in his life.

He had given the interview two days after being released. As she read what he'd had to say, Natasha felt her blood run cold.

*'I blame my wife. I loved her and the girl
I thought was my daughter. But then I
discovered she wasn't mine. It broke my
heart. I ran away as fast as I could go.'*

So her mother had betrayed her husband
and she, Natasha, was not his child. She
struggled to deny it, but lurking in her memory was a quarrel she had overheard between
them. Her father had shouted, 'Who was he?
Tell me!' And he'd called her mother some
terrible names. The next day he had gone.

Another memory returned—Jenson walking into the room as she was telling this story
to a fellow employee. How sympathetic he
had been, encouraging her to talk. How kind
she had thought him, while all the time he
was softening her up so that he could pounce
on her, while storing the information in case
it could be a useful weapon. That was his
way. He liked to have weapons against everyone.

Checking back, he'd found that one little item and made a note of it. Mario's action over the advertisements had convinced
him he had nothing left to gain, and still he'd
lashed out to hurt her for revenge.

Now she saw that years of being warned
not to trust men went back to this point. Her

mistrust had made her wary of Mario, but it was based on a lie. And that lie threatened the love they shared.

Unless she could find a way to solve the problem.

Suddenly she found words whispering through her head. *I have a faint cold fear thrills through my veins, That almost freezes up the heat of life.*

Juliet had spoken those words, faced with the decision that would change everything. And now Natasha felt the cold fear running through her. She must do something to make Mario return. But what?

'*She* will know,' she said. 'I'll go and ask her.'

Hurriedly, she flung on some clothes and rushed out of the room and downstairs.

Damiano was just crossing the hall. 'Just on my way to breakfast,' he said. 'No Mario?'

'He'll…be a while,' she stammered.

Damiano chuckled. 'Ah, still asleep, is he? I guess you must have exhausted him.'

She managed a smile. 'Something like that. I have to hurry away for a while.'

She quickly went out, seeing the hotel driver just outside. She approached him.

'Please take me to the Via Capello.'

In a moment they were away. She didn't

notice Giorgio standing in the doorway with a puzzled frown.

For the whole journey she sat tense, watching Verona glide past her, wondering what the city would mean to her in future. The place where she and her Romeo had achieved their happy ending? Or the place where the star-crossed lovers had been forced to accept that their love was never meant to be?

At last they drew up outside the Casa di Giulietta and she got out.

'Shall I wait for you?' the driver asked.

'No. I don't know how long I'll be. Thank you, but go back.'

He drove off, leaving her standing there. Then she went to the house, which had just opened for the day. A doorman greeted her, recognising her as a bride who was booked in a couple of days ahead.

'You'll find everything just as you're hoping for,' he called cheerfully.

'I'm sure I will,' she called back politely.

But would her wedding be as she was hoping for? Would anything in her life be right again?

As always, Juliet was standing in the courtyard. Natasha headed for the statue, glad that for the moment they were alone.

'I never asked your advice before,' she said.

'I believed you were just a fantasy. But now my whole world is upside down, and maybe you're the one person who can help me.

'What can I do? I made a silly mistake but I was confused. I didn't want to hurt Mario. I just couldn't understand what it would mean to him. Now he thinks I don't really love him, but I do. How can I make him believe that?'

Silence.

'Oh, please, you must help me. You know more about love than anyone. Tell me what I can do.'

She pressed her hand against her chest.

'You understand that, don't you?' she said to Juliet, who also had a hand on her breast. 'You know what it's like to press your hand over the pain, hoping to make it go away. But it doesn't go, and you become frantic trying to think of something that will help. I can't think of anything. What can I do?'

She took a step closer to Juliet, seeking to look her in the eye. She told herself not to be fanciful, otherwise she might have imagined Juliet's soft voice saying, *He's as troubled and unsure as you are.*

I know. He's suffering terribly and it's my fault. I thought the worst of every man because of my father, but now I realise that I shouldn't have done.

Discovering that you'd read the letter hurt him. He hasn't completely recovered.

Nor have I.

You're coping better than he is.

Truly? What can I do now?

Be kind to him. He is confused.

But what is it that confuses him?

You. You always have, although he would never admit it.

Does our love really have a future?

Who can tell? You can only hope.

And hope might come to nothing. That fact had to be faced. She would return to the hotel and find him not there because he no longer wanted her. It was over. He would never return.

Tears filled her eyes, blurring her vision so that the street around her seemed to become a swirling mass. She groped her way forward, missed the edge of the pavement and crashed to the ground. She was intensely aware of pain going through her head before she blacked out.

The first person Mario met on his return was Damiano.

'So there you are!' his brother exclaimed. 'I thought you were still upstairs, sleeping it off while Natasha was away.'

'Away?'

'She came downstairs a few hours ago. She went off somewhere in a hurry.'

'Went somewhere? You mean she's gone? Where?'

'She didn't say where she was going. Just walked out and didn't come back. You don't mean there's something wrong, surely? The two of you are getting married tomorrow. She's probably making last-minute preparations for the wedding.'

'Yes, of course,' Mario said in a voice that was deliberately blank to hide the storm of alarm that was rising within him.

'I expect she's preparing a special surprise for you.'

Yes, Mario thought desperately. Natasha was preparing a surprise for him, and he had a dreadful feeling that he knew what the surprise was.

'Oh, no!' he breathed. 'How could she do this to me?'

'What do you mean?' Damiano demanded.

'She's done it again.'

'Done what again?'

'What she did before—leaving without a goodbye, when I wasn't there to see. Disappearing into thin air like she'd never existed.'

'I'm sure you're wrong about that,' Damiano protested.

Mario tore his hair. 'You have no idea,' he raged. 'She vanished and I spent weeks looking for her before I realised that I'd never find her because she'd shut me out of her life.' His voice rose in anguish. *'Now she's done it again.'*

Nobody had noticed Giorgio entering the hall. He stood watching Mario with a puzzled frown.

'What's happened?' he asked at last.

'Have you seen Natasha today?' Mario demanded.

'Yes, I saw her get into the car with the chauffeur a few hours ago. He was only gone half an hour.'

'Fetch him,' Mario said.

Giorgio went out and returned with the chauffeur.

'Where did you take her?' Mario demanded.

'To the Via Capello.'

'And you brought her back?'

'No, she told me not to wait for her.'

'So she's gone,' Mario muttered. 'She's gone.'

He turned away so that they shouldn't see his face, which he knew must betray his pain, greater than any he'd known in his life before. He'd wanted so much to believe in her. Since their quarrel the night before he'd brooded over what lay before him. A life with her, always worried about the strength of her love? Or a life without her?

He'd paced the dark streets for hours, trying to understand his own heart. By the time he'd arrived home he knew that Natasha mattered more than anything in the world. However hard it was for him, he would do what he had to for their love to succeed; the thought of losing her was unbearable.

And he had arrived to find her gone.

He wanted to howl with rage, but even more with misery. She had betrayed his love, abandoned him, while knowing what it would do to him.

'Why don't you look in her room?' Damiano said. 'If she's really gone she'll have taken everything with her.'

'All right,' Mario said heavily.

What was the point? he thought. He would find her room deserted and the brutal truth underlined. Moving mechanically, he went up to her room and opened the door. Then he grew still.

The wardrobe was open, and inside it he

could see her clothes. Pulling open drawers, he found more clothing.

'She hasn't gone for good,' Damiano said, coming in behind him. 'Or she would never have left all this behind.'

'But where did she go?' Mario asked hoarsely.

'The chauffeur said he took her to the Via Capello,' Giorgio said. 'Surely she went to Juliet's house.'

'Yes,' Mario said at once. 'I understand that now.'

Everything was becoming clear to him. Natasha had gone to consult Juliet, and now she would know how the two of them could put things right.

One thing was clear. He must join her as soon as possible. He headed for the front door.

'Hey, Mario,' Giorgio called. 'Where are you going?'

Mario paused and looked back at him. 'I'm going to find my lady,' he said.

As he drove himself to the Via Capello the words haunted him, as they had many times before. *It is my lady. Oh, it is my love.*

'"Oh, that she knew she were,"' he murmured.

At last Juliet's house came in sight. He parked and ran down the street to the alley that led to the courtyard. There was no sign of Natasha. All he could see was Juliet, staring ahead, coolly indifferent to her surroundings. He placed himself in front of her.

'Was she here?' he demanded. 'Did she come to you and ask your help? Did you help her?'

No response. Nor had he expected one. Nobody else could help them now.

He wandered through the house, seeking her without success. In one room he stood looking around him, reflecting that this was where their wedding was supposed to take place, and wondering what the future held.

Once more he returned to Juliet. A small group of tourists had gathered in front of her, pleading for her attention.

'It's very tempting to talk to her, isn't it?' a woman said to Mario. 'We came here earlier and there was a lovely young woman talking to her as if it really mattered. But I don't think she had any luck because as soon as she left she got hurt.'

'Hurt? How?'

'I'm not sure what happened. She just seemed to lose her balance. She went down hard and hit her head on the pavement. The last I saw, she was being taken to the hospital.'

Barely able to speak, he forced himself to

say, 'You said she was a young woman. What did she look like?'

'Pretty, blue eyes, blonde hair.'

'And how did she seem?'

'Not sure, really. She wasn't moving. I suppose she might actually have been dead.'

He swallowed. 'Thank you for telling me,' he said hoarsely.

It took him ten minutes to get to the nearest hospital. There, he tore inside and up to the desk.

'A young woman was brought in this morning,' he gasped. 'She had a fall in the Via Capello. I must see her.'

The receptionist made a phone call and a nurse appeared.

He followed her into a small side ward and held his breath at the sight of Natasha lying on the bed. Her eyes were closed and it seemed to him that she was frighteningly still.

'Is this the person you are looking for?' the nurse asked.

'Yes, this is the person I was looking for.'

'Please tell me who she is.'

'Her name is Natasha Bates.'

'And who is her next of kin?'

'I am. I'm her husband. At least, I will be in a few days. If she lives.'

He had to force himself to say the last few

words, but the fear was more than he could endure.

'We don't yet know how seriously she's hurt,' the nurse said. 'She's still unconscious, but hopefully she'll soon come round.'

He moved to the bed, looking down at Natasha lying there. She seemed different to the strong, determined young woman he remembered: smaller, more frail and vulnerable.

A sudden fearsome echo haunted him: Romeo coming to Juliet in the tomb, seeing her lying there, silent and motionless, believing her dead. He tried to fight the thought away but he had a terrified feeling that she would leave him unless he could prevent her.

'Natasha,' he said, taking a chair beside the bed. 'It's me, darling. Can you hear me?'

She neither moved nor spoke.

'Are you there?' he begged. 'Please tell me that you're there.'

His heart sank. Her breathing told him that she was still alive, but in another sense she wasn't there. She was living in another universe, one where she might be trapped for ever.

'You went away from me once,' he whispered. 'I thought I would go mad at your rejection, but you came back and we found each other. Then today I thought you'd abandoned me again, and losing you was even worse than before.

'What happened was my fault. I couldn't bear discovering that I'd been living in a fantasy, that you loved me less than I'd thought. But if that's true—' he hesitated '—if the love is mainly on my side, then...then I'll live with that as long as I can have you. Do you understand? I'll accept any conditions as long as I don't lose you again. Even if—' he shuddered '—even if you never really wake up, but stay like this always, I won't leave you. I'll care for you and love you for years and years, until the day we can be finally together for ever.'

He leaned closer to murmur into her ear, 'Don't leave me. I'm yours in every way and I always will be. Natasha? Can you hear me?'

'Yes,' she whispered.

'I followed you all the way to Juliet's house. You went to ask her help, didn't you?'

'Yes.' She whispered the word so softly that he wasn't sure he'd heard properly.

'What?' he asked eagerly, leaning closer.

'She was very kind to me.'

He was suddenly sure that they understood each other. He must seize this moment, lest there should never be another.

'I tried too,' he said. 'But she stayed silent. I reckon she was telling me to see the truth for myself.' Inspiration came to him. 'And the truth we have to understand is that we love each other more than we can say in mere words. We've always known that, but we've never managed to face it before. But now the time has come and if I do nothing else in the world I have to make sure that you know.'

He kissed her again softly before murmuring, 'You are my lady. You are my love. Oh, that you knew you are.'

'Am I?' she whispered. 'Am I truly?'

'You know you are. And you will always know that you are.'

'How can I believe it? It's too good to be true.'

'Then I'll have to spend my life convincing you. I was so afraid you wouldn't wake up.'

'I was in such a strange place. I couldn't tell which way to turn, but suddenly you were there, beckoning me.'

'I always will be. I'll never let you go.'

The nurse appeared. She checked Natasha's pulse, read the machines and smiled at the result.

'This is what we hoped for,' she said. 'It's not serious. A few days' rest and you'll be back on your feet.'

When she had left they hugged, looking deep into each other's eyes, reading the depths for the first time. But now no words were spoken. No words were needed. Soon Natasha's eyes closed and Mario held her while she slept, thinking blissfully of the years ahead when he would hold her many times in his arms and always in his heart.

The wedding had to be delayed for two weeks, but at last the time came when they entered Juliet's house and made the vows of lifelong love and fidelity. Once, many years before, another couple had vowed the same, only to see their happiness cut short. But Natasha and Mario had no fear.

After the ceremony they went out onto the balcony, where Giorgio had arranged for a photographer to be clicking his camera madly. But the bride and groom were barely aware of him. They saw only each other.

'Just us,' he said as they held each other later that night.

'Not quite just us,' she murmured. 'There were two other people there. Couldn't you sense them?'

'Yes, they were there, watching over us as they've always done. And perhaps they always will.'

'No need,' she said. 'From now on we'll watch over each other.'

'Do you really think we can?'

'Yes, we can.' She turned in the bed, taking him in a fervent embrace.

'Come here,' she said. 'Come here *now*.'

* * * * *

SPECIAL EXCERPT FROM

HARLEQUIN®

Romance

Read on for an exclusive sneak preview of
EXPECTING THE EARL'S BABY
by *Jessica Gilmore*,
the first book in the enchanting
Harlequin® Romance trilogy
SUMMER WEDDINGS…

Seb's eyes darkened to an impenetrable green, a hint of something dangerous flickering at their core, and awareness shivered down Daisy's spine. She moved backward, just a few centimeters, almost propelled by the sheer force of his gaze until her back hit the wooden paneling. She leaned against it, thankful for the support, her legs weak.

She was still caught in his gaze. Warmth spread out from her abdomen, along her limbs, and her skin buzzed where his eyes rested on her, with the memory of his touch skittering along her nerves. Nervous, she licked her lips, the heat in her body intensifying as she watched his eyes move to her mouth, recognized the hungry expression in them.

He wanted a working marriage. A full marriage.

Right now, that seemed like the only thing that made sense in this whole tangled mess.

He took a step closer. And another. Daisy stayed still, almost paralyzed by the purposeful intent in his face, her pulse hammering an insistent beat of need, of want, at every pressure point in her body, a sweet, aching swelling in her chest.

"Seb?" It was almost a plea, almost a sob, a cry for something, an end to the yearning that so suddenly and so fiercely gripped her.

He paused, his eyes still on her. And then one last step. So close and yet still, still not touching even though her body was crying out for contact, pulled toward him by the magnetism of sheer need. He leaned, just a little, a hand on either side of her, braced against the wall.

He still hadn't touched her.

They remained perfectly still, separated by mere millimeters, their eyes locked, heat flickering between them, the wait stoking it higher and higher. He had to kiss her—had to—or she would spontaneously combust. He had to press that hard mouth against hers. To know her again. To fulfill her again.

He had to.

Don't miss Jessica Gilmore's stunning opening to the
SUMMER WEDDINGS *trilogy,*
EXPECTING THE EARL'S BABY.
Available April 2015 wherever
Harlequin Romance books and ebooks are sold.

www.Harlequin.com